groaned,

pulling the warning citation off her dorm room door.

"What's the matter?" Scott asked.

Faith handed Scott the citation so he could read it. "Liza left her candles burning again. She could have started a fire! And *I'm* the one who's going to get punished."

"But you didn't do anything," Scott protested.

"It doesn't matter," Faith said. "At least not to my resident adviser. It's a *room* violation, and I live in the room, so I share responsibility."

"That's not fair," Scott sympathized, putting his arms around Faith. "But don't worry. It can't be that bad."

Faith struggled free from Scott's grip. "How would you know?" she cried. "You're so slippery, you never get caught."

"Hey," Scott said, "this isn't my fault."

"Of course it's your fault," Faith ranted. "If I hadn't gotten in trouble for using a fake ID, I wouldn't have to worry about this now."

Faith knew she wasn't being logical, but she couldn't stop herself. "I should have known better than to give you another chance. Being with you only leads to one thing— trouble. Just please get out of here and out of my life before you make it even worse."

Don't miss these books
in the exciting FRESHMAN DORM series

FRESHMAN CHOICES

LINDA A. COONEY

HarperPaperbacks
A Division of HarperCollins Publishers

This is a work of fiction. The characters, incidents, and dialogues are products of the author's imagination and are not to be construed as real. Any resemblance to actual events or persons, living or dead, is entirely coincidental.

HarperPaperbacks *A Division of* HarperCollins*Publishers*
10 East 53rd Street, New York, N.Y. 10022.

Cover art by Tony Greco

First printing: December 1991

Printed in the United States of America

HarperPaperbacks and colophon are trademarks of HarperCollins*Publishers*

10 9 8 7 6 5 4 3 2 1

One

"There you are!" KC Angeletti cried as Faith Crowley opened the door to the roof of her dorm, Coleridge Hall. "We've been sweltering up here, waiting to find out what happened to you."

"Yeah," said Winnie Gottlieb, jumping up from her psychedelic beach towel and rushing forward to put a protective arm around Faith. "I wish you had let us come with you. What did they do? Were you really scared? How many of them were there? Did they let you speak in your own defense?"

Though Faith had just had the worst day of her life, she had to laugh. In the past five seconds, motormouth Winnie had asked her almost as many questions as the University of Springfield peer review board that had just interrogated her. Only Faith hadn't been laughing then. It had been all she could do to keep from bursting into tears as she waited for the hammer of justice to come crashing down on her head.

"Sit down, Faith," Winnie said, running back to her beach towel and patting a spot beside her. "Tell us everything."

Faith squinted in the harsh glare of the sun overhead. She could barely see her friends through the heat lines that emanated from the roof, blurring the distant mountaintops. It had to be at least ninety degrees, and with each step, her sneakers sank into the sticky tar. She was grateful to sit down beside Winnie. Her whole body was slick with sweat, causing her white T-shirt and denim cut-off shorts to stick to her uncomfortably. But this discomfort was nothing compared to what she'd gone through in the past week and a half.

Recently, Faith had been nabbed by a campus security guard at a local bar. Even though she was only eighteen, too young to drink alcohol in this western state, she'd tried to buy beer with a fake ID. The security guard had slapped her with a citation, which meant she'd had to appear before a peer review board. Faith was still in shock just thinking about it. She'd always been so responsible, so well behaved. She'd never gotten in trouble for anything in her life. But now she wasn't just guilty of breaking campus rules—she'd committed a crime!

"So?" Winnie asked, peering at Faith through her Mickey Mouse sunglasses. She wore a red Lycra bikini top, and purple-and-green striped Lycra running shorts that showed off her compact, muscular body. Her brown hair, which usually stuck straight up in spikes all over her head, had wilted in the heat, and her cheerful, animated face was flushed. "Tell us everything!"

"Yes," said KC, who lounged on a straw mat a few feet away, filing her nails. "No matter how bad it is, we're here for you." KC's long, slender legs glistened with suntan oil, and her long dark hair was pulled back into a loose ponytail. Her beautiful face with its high cheekbones was half hidden behind a pair of black sunglasses, and her perfect figure was displayed in a black two-piece swimsuit.

Faith was so grateful her two best friends from home had also chosen U. of S. Faith, Winnie, and KC had been inseparable since junior high school, back in Jacksonville, but now Faith needed their friendship and support more than ever.

"I was petrified," Faith confessed as KC and

Winnie edged closer to listen. "They made me sit on a chair in the middle of the room, while three of them sat at this long table, staring at me. I felt like a criminal, which I guess I am."

"But what did they do to you?" Winnie asked. "What's your punishment?"

Faith gulped some water from Winnie's plastic squeeze bottle to soothe her parched throat. "I'm on probation," she said in a hoarse voice.

"What does that mean?" KC asked, lowering her sunglasses and focusing her gray eyes on Faith.

"It means I have to be on perfect behavior until the day we graduate," Faith said. "I can't even step one foot inside a bar in town, or I'll get another citation. If I want to participate in any extracurricular activities, I have to get approval from the dean first."

"And what happens if you do something wrong?" Winnie asked. "Not that you're going to."

"You bet I'm not," Faith said. "If I get cited for even a minor infraction, I'll have to go before the board again, and they could really pounce on me, like call in my parents for a conference. And if I get cited for another *major* infraction, like alcohol, they could kick me out of school."

"Wow," KC breathed, shaking her head. "That's so unfair. You just made one mistake."

"My one and only," Faith vowed. "You thought I

was a goody-goody before, wait 'til you see me now. I never want to hear the word *citation* for as long as I live. In fact, can I borrow your nail scissors?" Faith asked KC, glancing at the open leather manicure case on KC's towel.

"What for?" asked KC.

Faith pulled her fake ID card out of the pocket of her shorts. "It's time to destroy this, once and for all."

Faith stared at her fake University of Springfield ID card. Her own face stared back at her, the smile defiant, the brown eyes scared behind a curtain of brown hair. The hair color wasn't hers. Faith's long, straight hair was usually honey blond. She'd dyed it just for the photograph. The name on the card wasn't hers either. Faith had tried to pass herself off as twenty-one-year-old senior, Cheryl White.

To think she'd gone to all that trouble just to impress a guy. What a fool she'd been. The guy hadn't even been worth it. Sure, Scott Sills was cute. Adorable even. And so free, so happy to be alive. Faith had wanted to prove to him that she could be as wild and uninhibited as he was. But he'd abandoned her in the bar as soon as he'd seen the security guard. All he cared about was saving his own skin.

"Thanks," Faith said, taking the scissors from

KC's outstretched hand. She cut a jagged line right through the middle of her photograph, then hacked the plastic card into tiny pieces.

"Whoa!" Winnie observed. "Leave something for the vultures."

"I just wish I had a magnifying glass," Faith said, stabbing at the soft tar roof with one of the plastic shards. "I'd set the whole pile on fire. Meanwhile, I'm going to read the student handbook cover to cover and memorize every rule and regulation." Faith pulled a purple-and-gold paperback out of her book bag and opened it to the first page.

"How many rules are there?" Winnie asked, taking the squeeze bottle and pouring water on top of her head.

"Tons," Faith answered. "This book is eighty pages long."

"Really?" KC asked, taking the handbook from Faith and flipping through it. "I know everyone got one of these books at orientation, but I never really read it."

"You should," Faith counseled, "so you don't get into trouble the way I did."

"Couldn't you just give us the abbreviated version?" Winnie asked. "Like, 'Three Short Steps to a More Obedient You.'"

"Let's see," Faith said, trying to remember. "There

are the really obvious ones, like no alcohol on dorm premises. That's a major infraction. Then there are minor infractions, which are usually dorm violations. Those won't put you in front of the board unless you're on probation, like me, in which case even one tiny mistake can get you in big trouble."

"Look at all this stuff," KC exclaimed, reading from the handbook. "You're not allowed to put anything on the walls. No pets. No burning candles or extension cords. You can't even make an extra key to someone else's room."

Winnie held out her hands in front of her. "Handcuff me right now. It sounds as if I've broken every rule in the book. Why should Faith be the only one to suffer for her sins? I'm willing to pay my debt to society. Just don't make me give back my key to Josh's room." Josh Gaffey, Winnie's boyfriend, was a computer major who lived down the hall from her in the jock dorm, Forest Hall.

"You have a key to Josh's room?" Faith asked. "I didn't know that."

Winnie shrugged. "It's no big deal."

"Sounds like a big deal to me," KC said. "That's almost like living together."

Winnie squirted water all over her legs and arms, then flapped them frantically in a passing breeze. "We're not ready for *that* yet, but I have to say things are pretty stable right now. Did you ever think that word would apply to me? Stable? I mean, how many years have I spent bouncing around from guy to guy, or bouncing off the walls . . ."

"Or just bouncing," Faith said, amazed Winnie had the energy to move around so vigorously in this heat.

"But look at me now," Winnie said, rolling over onto her stomach and rubbing her sweaty forehead against the beach towel. "I've been going out with the same guy for almost a year—not counting the times we broke up—but we've been tight now for months. I guess you could say we're like an old married couple."

"I envy you," KC said, gazing at the faraway mountains. "My relationship with Peter could end any minute."

KC's boyfriend, Peter Dvorsky, was a photography major who lived on the first floor of Coleridge Hall. He was also the first guy KC had ever loved. Peter had just made the final cut in the Morgan Foundation photo contest. If he won, he'd leave U. of S. immediately for a year of travel and study in Europe.

"Has Peter heard anything yet?" Winnie asked.

"No," KC said, unleashing a heavy sigh. "But he's going to win. I just know it. He's too talented not to."

Faith nodded. "But even if he does go away, it's

only for a year."

"Only?" KC clutched her stomach and groaned. "I don't know how I'll survive even a week without him."

"You won't be alone," Winnie said, putting her arm around KC and laying her head on KC's shoulder. "You'll always have us."

Faith looked at her friends with a mixture of affection and amazement. The last thing she'd expected when she started at U. of S. was that she'd be the only one of the three who wasn't involved in an intense, committed relationship. Faith had come to college with her boyfriend of four years, Brooks Baldwin. KC, on the other hand, had been far more interested in her business courses and getting into the Tri Beta sorority than in finding romance. And Winnie had been too scattered and flaky to focus on any one guy. But now both of them were seriously involved, and Faith was on her own.

She was beginning to think that maybe she hadn't appreciated Brooks in the end. Not that she wanted him back—she was even getting used to the idea that Brooks was now engaged to Winnie's roommate, Melissa McDormand. It was more what Brooks represented: comfort, predictability, reliability. He was the sort of person you could always count on, no matter what. And Faith was learning people like that were hard to find.

"Have you heard from Scott?" Winnie asked, moving away from KC and dribbling water onto Faith's bare stomach.

"No," Faith said as the cool water ran down her hot skin. "He said he wanted to make up for what he'd done. He said he was going to prove to me that he wasn't so bad after all. But then he disappeared again."

"What a jerk," KC said, filing her nails with quick, angry strokes.

Faith had to agree. Scott was the opposite of Brooks in every way. It didn't matter that he was cute, bubbly, and made her laugh. It didn't matter that she felt happy and light and free when she was with him. He'd deserted her when she needed him most.

"It's okay," Faith assured her friends. "I've learned from all this. And I've figured out a foolproof plan so I never get involved with another jerk again."

"Oh yeah?" Winnie asked, picking up her copy of *Fitness* magazine and fanning herself frenetically. "If it works, I'll bet you could write a book and make a lot of money."

"I just hope it works for me," Faith said. "It's called 'Operation Mr. Right.' I've made a mental checklist of all the qualities I'm looking for in a guy.

He has to be solid and dependable like Brooks, but fun and spontaneous like Scott. Not to mention handsome, intelligent, and considerate."

KC paused in her nail filing and her expression grew soft. "I'd say that sounds impossible, except that I found someone just like that in Peter."

"That's exactly my point," Faith said, picking up a burning tube of sunscreen from Winnie's towel and opening it gingerly. "Until I find a guy with every single quality on my list, I'm not even going to go on one date."

"Sounds good to me," KC said. "Why set yourself up to be disappointed again?"

"Playing by the rules saves a lot of time and trouble," Faith said, "and these days I don't have time to be miserable, anyway. There's that big production of *Macbeth* coming up, and I'm hoping to be on the stage crew. Plus, we've got that big Western Civ midterm, and I haven't even started studying for it yet."

"Me neither," Winnie said.

"I don't even know *what* to study," said KC, who was also in the class. "At least you two are going in with A averages. Mine's closer to a C. I don't suppose you guys would want to cram for this together?"

"Why not?" Winnie said. "We can get Lauren to work with us, too." Lauren Turnbell-Smythe used to be Faith's roommate, but now she lived off campus. Lauren was in the same Western Civilization section as Faith, Winnie, and KC.

"You can invite Peter and Josh," Faith said. "Don't leave them out just because *I'm* unattached."

"How about Thursday?" KC asked, opening her leather-bound datebook.

Before Faith or Winnie could answer, the door to the roof opened and a reed-thin young woman appeared. She was dressed all in black, creating a striking contrast with her dead white skin. Her eyes were pale blue, and her straight black hair was rolled into a neat french twist. Faith recognized the icy beauty as Erin Grant, a junior and a drama major. Come to think of it, Erin had auditioned for the segment of the U. of S. Follies Faith had directed a couple of months back, and Faith hadn't given her a part. Erin had a certain stage presence, but her singing voice was low and affected, just like her speaking voice.

"Hi, Erin," Faith called out. "Coming to sunbathe?"

"Hardly," Erin said in the throaty, clipped tones Faith remembered. "I'm here to tell you to get off the roof."

Winnie tipped her Mickey Mouse sunglasses just

low enough so Faith could see her roll her eyes. Faith felt the same way.

"Why should we get off the roof?" Faith asked, trying not to show the irritation she was feeling.

"Because I'm the new Resident Adviser," Erin informed them. "And if you don't do what I tell you, I'll give you a citation."

Citation! The word rocked Faith like a nuclear explosion. It didn't matter how much Erin got on her nerves. If Erin had the power to get her kicked out of school, then Faith was going to make sure she stayed on Erin's good side.

"We were just leaving," Faith said, jumping to her feet and pulling the beach mat out from under Winnie. "I didn't know being on the roof is a violation. Is it in the handbook?"

"Page sixty-seven," Erin said. "Subsection b."

"What happened to Beverly Brandt?" KC asked coolly, rising from her towel. "Didn't she used to be the R.A. in Coleridge?"

"Beverly's traveling around the country with a young people's orchestra for the rest of the semester," Erin said. "I'm taking her place. But I'm not going to be as lax as she was. Starting from now on, this place is going to be run by the book."

"I hear you," Faith said. "We've got to follow the rules." Faith hated the way she was sucking up to

Erin, but she had to. If she sounded cooperative, maybe Erin wouldn't give her another citation.

"Exactly," Erin said. "And that's the whole reason I came up here in the first place. Faith, there's a radio blasting in your room. That's another violation."

"It's my roommate's," Faith explained. "I don't even own a radio."

"It doesn't matter whose radio it is," Erin said, leveling her icy stare at Faith. "Both roommates are equally responsible for the condition of their room."

"Okay, I'll go downstairs and turn it off," Faith said, rolling up the straw beach mat as she headed for the door.

"Not so fast," Erin said, pointing to the little pile of plastic shards that had once been Faith's fake ID. "Littering's also a violation. That makes three in the past five minutes. If you don't clean up your act, Faith, I am going to give you a citation."

Faith gulped. *My life is over!* she thought miserably as she raced to pick up every last bit of plastic.

"This won't ever happen again," Faith said. "Please don't give me a citation."

"Well, I won't this time," Erin said, to Faith's great relief. "But I'll be watching you. I'll be watching you very closely from now on."

Two

"Splash me again, Brooks," Melissa McDormand murmured lazily. Winnie's roommate lay on her stomach, beside Brooks, on the gray wooden raft that floated in the middle of Mill Pond. Her blue racer-back swimsuit showed off her taut, lean runner's body, which was dusted all over with light brown freckles. Her coppery red hair glinted in the glaring sunlight.

Brooks gazed lovingly down at his fiancée. Her freckled face looked so peaceful and relaxed.

Maybe it was the gentle bobbing of the raft in the murky green water that calmed her. Maybe it was the cool breeze that wafted, occasionally, from the mountains, rustling the branches of the willow trees that ringed the pond. Brooks wished Melissa could always be this way, but he had a feeling her expression would change when he told her his news.

His dad and stepmom were coming to Springfield for a visit, and they wanted to meet their future in-laws, Melissa's parents. Brooks knew Melissa would resist this idea with every ounce of strength she had. Melissa was ashamed of her parents. Her father, an unemployed hotel doorman, was an alcoholic who hadn't left his house in years. Melissa's mother was a housekeeper. Brooks had never even met them, though they lived right here in Springfield, just a few minutes from campus.

Brooks had to figure out a way to break down Melissa's defenses. He had to make Melissa see that there was nothing to be afraid of. His parents were nice people. They would accept Melissa and her family no matter how poor they were.

"Brooks!" Melissa begged, opening one brown eye. "Please splash me! It's so hot!"

The news could wait a few minutes. Brooks wanted to enjoy himself a little longer. He leaned down so that his face was just inches from Melissa's. "Are you saying you want to get wet?" he asked. "I want to make sure I understood you."

"You understand me perfectly," Melissa said.

"Okay," Brooks said. With one swift motion, he scooped Melissa up in his strong arms and dumped her into the rippling green water.

"Brooks!" Melissa screamed, when her head bobbed above the surface.

Brooks jumped off the raft and felt the cool water envelop him. Then he floated onto his back and kicked a huge spray at Melissa. "You said you wanted to get wet," he teased.

"Two can play at that game," Melissa said, ducking beneath the water.

A second later, Brooks felt her arms wrap around his waist and drag him under. Brooks easily broke her grasp, pulling her up above the water. "Race you!" he challenged.

"How far?" Melissa asked, her face already assuming the ready expression Brooks had seen many times before. It was the same look of stony concentration she had prior to running her record-setting 440 races for the U. of S. women's track team or when she studied for a final in one of her killer premed courses. But track star or no, she was no match for him in the water, especially when he had so much nervous energy from the problem on his mind.

"To the beach," Brooks said, pointing to a stretch of sand fifty yards away. "Any style."

"One, two, three, go!" Melissa shouted, her lean body arching above the water like a dolphin, her arms raised above her head as she started the butterfly stroke.

Brooks opted for the crawl, his powerful legs propelling him through the water like an outboard motor. Adrenaline surged through his body, and he felt his heart pound in his chest as he overtook her. But Melissa's competitive spirit gave her new energy, and she stayed right alongside him until their knees hit the sandy bottom of the shallow water.

"Tie!" Brooks proclaimed. He grabbed Melissa, carried her slippery body to the shore, and dropped her gently in the sand. Then he flopped down beside her and pulled her on top of him.

"Oh, worthy opponent," Melissa said softly.

"I'm not your opponent," Brooks whispered, looking at her with intense longing. "I'll always be on your side."

Their eyes locked for an instant, then Brooks pulled her to him and pressed his lips against hers, his fingers entwining in her wet hair. Melissa kissed him back with a raw passion he'd never felt before. They rolled over and over on the beach, oblivious of the sand covering every inch of their bodies.

At last they broke apart and lay together, on their backs, holding hands. High above their heads, a flock of birds flew in a V pattern against the cloud-less, light blue sky. The moment was so perfect, Brooks didn't want to spoil it by mentioning his parents' visit.

Brooks understood why ambitious, striving Melissa wanted to make a better life for herself than her parents had. But she couldn't hide from her family, or hide them from the world. And she certainly couldn't hide them from his parents, especially since the two of them were planning to get married. This was too important. This was something that had to be faced. Even if Melissa blew up at him, Brooks had to say something.

"Uh, Melissa . . ." Brooks said, biting his lip. "You'll never guess who's coming to visit a week from Sunday."

"Who?" Melissa asked, moving closer to Brooks and crossing one leg over his.

"My dad and stepmom."

Melissa didn't say anything, but Brooks could feel the tension in her fingers. "And?"

This was the hard part. The part Melissa wouldn't want to hear. "And they want to meet your parents," Brooks said, bracing himself for Melissa's reaction.

"What's the rush?" Melissa asked, her voice tight and constricted. "We haven't even set a date yet."

"I know, I know," Brooks said comfortingly, stroking her hand. "And it doesn't have to be anything major. My parents just want to take your parents out for a nice dinner and say hello. We thought we'd go to Moreno's."

"Moreno's?" Melissa practically shouted as she shot straight up. "You can't take my parents there!"

"Why not?" Brooks asked, sitting up so he could face Melissa. "It's a very nice restaurant."

"That's not the point."

"Then what is?"

Melissa's nostrils flared as she took in a deep breath.

"Well?" Brooks asked.

Melissa fixed her angry brown eyes upon him. "The point," she said, "is that you don't have to take care of everything all the time. I'm a capable person, too. I can certainly arrange a dinner for our parents."

"What difference does it make who arranges it?" Brooks asked. "It's all the same thing."

"It's *not* the same," Melissa insisted, brushing the sand off her legs with sharp, rapid strokes. "*I* want to do it. By myself. Without any help from you."

"But Melissa. . ." Brooks protested.

"Either I do it, or the dinner's off," Melissa said firmly, jumping to her feet.

Brooks stared up at her in frustration. Her long, lean body blocked the sun, and her face was in silhouette so he couldn't read its expression. But Brooks knew it held stubborn resolve. If Brooks wanted his parents to meet hers, he'd have to do it her way.

"Fine," Brooks said, with a shrug. "Whatever you want. If you want to plan the dinner, go ahead."

Liza Ruff wrapped her maroon velvet robe more tightly around her generous body and held the letter up to the light of the dripping candles scattered around the room.

"They met me in the day of success," she read aloud, in a booming voice, *"and I have learned by the perfect's report they have more in them than mortal knowledge."*

No. That wasn't right. She sounded too brassy. Not at all like an aristocrat's wife and the future Queen of Scotland. Liza, Faith's roommate, put down the blank piece of typewriter paper she'd been pretending to read from and moved in front of the electric fan that was whirring in her dormitory room.

The air fluttered Liza's collection of self-portraits that she'd tacked above her bed. Some were photographs of her starring in U. of S. and high school productions; a few were caricatures featuring scrawling orange curlicues for hair and big red lips that took up half the face. Along the side wall, at the foot of Liza's bed, was her collection of shoes—platform sandals with two-inch wooden soles, gold lamé pumps with three-inch heels, and a dozen other pairs with equally high heels that were impossible to walk in, but so flattering to the leg.

Liza had been up since 6:00 A.M., preparing for her audition for the U. of S. Drama Guild's new production of *Macbeth*. The audition wasn't for another week, but Liza still had a lot of work to do. She hadn't fully memorized her speech, and she still hadn't gotten fully inside the character. Hence the velvet robe and candle light, which she felt were crucial in helping her capture Lady Macbeth's overwhelming ambition.

There was nothing she wouldn't do to impress Lawrence Briscoe, the famous British director who was coming all the way from the Royal Shakespeare Academy in London just to direct this production. If Liza got the part of Lady Macbeth, maybe Briscoe would invite her back to England with him to start a career as a celebrated, *serious* actress.

"How do you do, Your Majesty?" Liza said with a flutey, snooty British accent, bowing low before an imaginary queen.

But that was just playing the clown again. Liza was all through with that. When she'd first arrived at U. of S. in the middle of the year, she'd made her mark more as a comedienne. She'd joked and strutted her way through the U. of S. Follies and the Crisis Hotline Benefit to great acclaim. But the problem was, people only saw her as someone who made them laugh or someone to laugh at.

Recently, Liza had been forced to realize that people saw her as a joke even when she wasn't performing. She'd overheard students saying her hair was the color of cheddar cheese and that her body was as fat as the Goodyear blimp. They'd ridiculed her clothes, her voice, her whole personality. It had been mortifying to hear, but even that was nothing compared to the fact that her roommate, Faith, couldn't stand her.

Liza sank onto her fluffy white down comforter and stared at Faith's neatly organized desk. There had to be at least ten framed snapshots of Faith and all her friends arranged in one corner.

Faith and her two best friends from home, Winnie and KC, eating bean curd at KC's family's health food restaurant.

Faith and Brooks Baldwin, her ex-boyfriend, sitting on a wall in front of their high school, wearing matching blue jeans with matching rips in the knees.

Faith and her old roommate, Lauren Turnbell-Smythe, sitting on the floor of this very room, stuffing handfuls of popcorn into each other's mouths.

Faith had so many friends without even trying. People just seemed to flock to her. And Faith could be so warm and giving. She was always willing to listen to other people's problems, even when her own life wasn't going well.

All Liza wanted was for Faith to treat her the same way, to make her feel as if she counted, that she was a real friend, not just a roommate Faith had gotten stuck with. Faith was such a naturally nice person that if Faith didn't like Liza, no one would. Faith was like a litmus test.

And so far, Liza had failed. Whenever Liza walked into the room, Faith froze up. She became tense and silent, as if she couldn't wait for Liza to leave. The only words that came out of her mouth were orders. *Turn down the boom box! Get rid of the coffee maker! Hide the fan!*

Liza had tried everything she could think of to get Faith to like her. She'd signed up for some of the same drama classes so they'd have something to talk about. She'd done favors for Faith's friends. She'd even tried to fix Faith up with an adorable guy, Scott Sills. Nothing had worked.

But Liza hadn't given up yet. She had one more

trick up her sleeve. Part of the problem was that Faith saw her the way everybody else did—as someone not to be taken seriously. That was all going to change, though. In fact, it was already changing.

Liza moved in front of the full-length mirror and studied her reflection, which flickered in the candlelight. She hadn't lost any weight yet, but she'd put a new rinse on her mop of curly hair. It was still red, but it was a more natural, reddish brown shade. She'd toned down her makeup, too, going lighter on the white face powder and switching her bright red lipstick for a more subtle shade of peach.

"Meet the new Liza Ruff!" Liza announced, raising her arms above her head. Then Liza noticed she was wearing her fuzzy pink bunny slippers, with little ears poking up at the front and white cotton tails at the back.

"So, I still need work," Liza said to herself as she kicked off the slippers. But she'd succeed, ultimately. She had to. Once Faith realized Liza was a serious actress, Faith would take her seriously, too. And once Faith respected her, could friendship be far behind?

But before she could win Faith's respect, she had to get the part of Lady Macbeth.

"When I burned in desire to question them further," she said, picking up the blank piece of paper again and pretending to read.

Liza's performance was interrupted by a knock on the door.

"Who is it?" Liza asked, pulling open the thick window curtains to let the daylight in.

"Scott Sills. Is Faith there?"

Liza's first impulse was to answer no and send Scott on his way. It wasn't as if Faith wanted to see him. Scott, a varsity player on the unbeaten U. of S. volleyball team, had ditched Faith at The Pub the night she'd gotten caught with her fake ID.

Then Liza had another thought. Faith had mentioned Scott wanted her to give him another chance. And even though Faith had claimed that she didn't care about Scott anymore, Liza suspected that Faith was still attracted to him. Maybe all Faith needed was a little push in Scott's direction.

Liza had nothing to lose and everything to gain by giving that push. Faith still blamed Liza for introducing her to Scott in the first place and for all the trouble that had resulted. But if Liza could help patch things up between them, Faith might forgive her. Then Faith would have a second reason to like Liza. Liza was beginning to like this picture of herself—a talented, soon-to-be-famous actress who still found the time to make her friends happy.

"Hello?" Scott knocked again. "Anybody home?"

"Just a minute!" Liza called, peeling off her heavy

robe and pulling on a pair of capri pants and a midriff halter top. She threw open the door and gave Scott a big smile. "Come in!"

Scott entered the room, carrying a football. He was tall, over six feet, and wore a cut-off football jersey and ripped denim shorts that showed off his tan, muscular body. His blond hair was long and shaggy and his amber eyes were questioning.

"Is Faith here?" he asked.

"Well, not in so many words," Liza said, pulling out her desk chair and gesturing for him to sit. "But she should be back any minute, if you want to wait."

Scott shrugged and pulled the chair directly in front of the fan. "Hope you don't mind if I hog your breeze," he said, closing his eyes and tilting his sweaty face so that the whirring air washed over it. "Mmmm," he sighed, shaking his head. "I'm glad I stopped by." Then he looked around the room, taking in the burning candles, which were dripping hot wax. "Having a seance?" he asked. "How 'bout bringing back Knute Rockne or Vince Lombardi? They could give my touch football team some pointers."

"So you play football, too?" Liza asked, trying to act impressed.

"Not really. It's just for fun. So where did you say Faith was?"

"I didn't," Liza said, noting the anxiety in his

eyes. Actually, she didn't have the slightest idea where Faith was, but she was hoping that if she kept him here long enough she'd think of some way to get the two of them back together.

"So tell me, Scott," Liza said, pulling up Faith's desk chair so that she could face him. "What's the latest on you two?"

"Unfortunately, nothing," Scott said, slumping a little. "I guess she's still really mad about what happened at The Pub?"

Scott said it more like a question, and Liza could tell he was hoping she might provide him with some information. This was the chance Liza had been waiting for. If she could convince him that there was still some hope for him with Faith, then she was halfway there.

"Well, of course Faith's not going to let you off the hook right away," Liza hedged, "but if you give her a little time, things might work out."

Scott leaned forward eagerly and clutched his football so tightly his tan fingers turned white. "Do you really think so? I tried to tell her that it wasn't completely my fault. I mean, I didn't tell her to get a fake ID, or anything. She acted as if she did that kind of thing all the time."

"Oh, I know," Liza agreed. "Nobody had to twist her arm."

"But of course I shouldn't have left her like that, all alone with the security guard. I should have figured out some way to help her."

"You meant well," Liza said, patting his knee.

Scott extended his long legs and leaned back in his chair. "I just wish I knew how to get her to like me again," he said, pounding on his football with one fist. "She's such a special girl. I'd really like to spend more time with her. But I guess I shouldn't be telling you this, right? You're her roommate, so you probably hate me, too."

"Of course I don't hate you!" Liza said. "I want to help."

Scott smiled. "Thanks. But I don't know if there's anything anyone can do at this point. I'll bet Faith wouldn't even have let me in if she'd been here. That's why I haven't come over before now. I didn't have the nerve."

"Maybe you have to catch her off guard," Liza suggested. "Don't give her a chance to shut you out."

"But how?" Scott asked. "I almost never run into her on campus. I keep hoping I'll bump into her accidentally but—"

"That's it!" Liza said, slapping one of Scott's long legs in her excitement. "We'll have to arrange an 'accidental' meeting."

Scott began to look a little hopeful. "Any ideas?"

"I have more than an idea," Liza said. "I have a time and a place. They're posting the sign-up sheet for *Macbeth* this Thursday at two o'clock in the dorm recreation center. They're holding the auditions there, too, because the University Theater's being renovated. I know Faith wants to work crew on the show. I'll make sure she shows up there at exactly two o'clock."

"I get it!" Scott said, his face lighting up. "Then I'll happen to wander by, and the rest is history!"

"Hopefully," Liza warned him. "It still might take some work."

"I'm willing to do whatever it takes," Scott said, standing up to leave. "I messed up, and I'm going to make it up to her. Thanks a lot, Liza. You don't know how much this means to me."

Tossing his football up in the air and catching it, Scott left the room whistling.

As Liza watched him go, she couldn't help feeling an ache inside. In her entire life, no one had ever felt that strongly about her or seemed so excited about seeing her. And maybe no one ever would.

Three

So Prince Henry of Portugal never sent his explorers all the way to Asia," Winnie said, Thursday afternoon. She lay sprawled on the dorm green, reviewing her scribbled Western Civ class notes, her face shaded by a hot pink umbrella hat. "They only got as far as the coast of West Africa."

"Then why did they call him Henry the Navigator?" asked Lauren Turnbell-Smythe, her violet eyes confused behind her round, wire-rimmed glasses. "He really didn't get too far."

"I don't know," Winnie said. "What do you think, KC?"

"Hmmmm?" KC asked dreamily. She knew she should be focusing on Western Civ, but she was far more aware of the firm pressure of Peter's back, pressing against hers, as they sat supporting each other. He felt so warm, so alive, so *solid*. It was hard to believe that one day soon he might vanish, leaving her all alone.

KC reached backward, just to reassure herself that, at least for the moment, he was still there. Peter's fingers laced through hers instantly, and KC felt a pain in her chest. If only there were some way to fuse their bodies together so they'd never have to be separated. But that was just being selfish.

"KC . . ." Winnie sang her name. Winnie was barely dressed in a red bikini top with a pair of neon green running shorts, but no one else on the vast, gently sloping lawn wore much more. The temperature had hit ninety for the fourth day in a row, and bathing suits seemed to be the most popular style of clothing.

"I'm sorry," KC said, reluctantly taking her hands back from Peter. "Where were we?"

"Henry the Navigator," said Josh Gaffey, who sat in the shade of a nearby tree, his knees buried under hundreds of connected sheets of computer paper. His longish, dark brown hair grazed the collar of his wrinkled, untucked T-shirt, which he wore over a pair of baggy shorts. He wore a tiny blue earring in his left ear, and a woven leather bracelet around his lank wrist.

KC felt badly that Josh, who wasn't even studying Western Civ, was paying more attention to their review session than she was. She felt even worse because she was the one who'd suggested they all study together in the first place. But how could she focus on the travelers of five hundred years ago when Peter might soon be going much farther than any of them had? In a way, KC almost wished she and Peter had lived back then, when people had never heard of airplanes and jet fuel.

"Okay," Winnie said, closing her notebook. "I know when I'm licked. Why don't we take a study break?"

She rolled over the grass toward Josh and tickled the bottoms of his bare feet. Josh merely tucked his feet under him and kept on working.

"That'll give Faith a chance to get here," Lauren said. "I wonder what's keeping her?"

"Did I hear 'study break?'" Peter asked, flinging his History of Art textbook aside. He backed up so that he was facing KC, then he lifted her up and sat her in his lap crosswise.

KC wrapped her arms around Peter's neck and stared at his face. She'd been doing that a lot lately, in an attempt to memorize it. Not that Peter's features were what was special about him. His hair color was somewhere between brown and blond. His eyes were hazel. He had a nose, a mouth, a chin, but nothing stood out. It was what happened when you put them all together. They added up to Peter, and KC wanted to sear the memory into her mind so she'd never forget.

When KC was alone, it was easier to convince herself that she could survive when he went away. But seeing him up close only made her realize how much she was kidding herself.

"Oh, Peter!" KC cried, covering his face with kisses and squeezing him tight. "What am I going to do without you?"

Though KC had sworn not to break down in front of him, she could already feel the tears welling up inside her, as they had every night since she'd discovered the letter from the Morgan Foundation in Peter's room, telling him he was one of the three finalists.

Peter pulled KC even closer and buried his head in her shoulder. "Don't even think about it," he murmured.

"This is such torture," KC groaned, stroking his fine, silky hair. "This waiting. This feeling like any minute the axe is going to drop. How much longer until you know?"

"I heard the final letters are going to arrive some-time this week," Peter said.

"And then you'll be on your way to a big career as a famous photographer," KC said, forcing herself to sound cheerful. "We'll have to have a big party to celebrate."

Peter deserved this break. He'd worked hard at photography all his life. True, he was only nine-teen, but already some of his portraits showed as much artistry and feeling as anything KC had seen in photography magazines. Soon, the whole world would know it.

"Leaving you is nothing to celebrate," Peter said, his face anguished. "I wish I could pack you in my suitcase and take you with me."

KC and Peter clung to each other as if any minute a strong wind might blow them apart.

"Now that's true love," Lauren said to Winnie. "Looking back, I realize I never had that with Dash."

KC felt another pang of guilt. Lauren was just as miserable as she was right now, but KC had been so wrapped up in her own problem that she'd com-pletely forgotten.

"Dash loved you," KC assured Lauren over Peter's shoulder. "Even if things didn't work out in the end, he did love you."

Dash Ramirez, a junior, had been Lauren's boyfriend until they'd gotten into a fight over an article they were co-writing for the college paper, *The Weekly Journal*. They'd each done terrible, hurtful things to the other, and now they weren't even speaking.

Lauren tore up clumps of grass and shredded them into tiny flecks. "It's weird," she said, sifting the grass between her fingers, "but I can hardly remember the good parts anymore. All I feel is pain."

"And I'm sure it just makes it harder that you still have to work with him," KC sympathized.

"Greg didn't realize what he was doing when he assigned Dash and me to write that His and Hers column," Lauren said. Greg Sukimaki was editor in chief of the *Journal*. "Now I have to deal with Dash every single day. But every word we say is strictly work-related. We don't even say hello or good-bye."

"How can love just disappear like that?" KC wondered, clutching Peter tightly. Were feelings really that temporary, like puffs of smoke? Lauren and Dash were still on the same campus, and they'd split up. What would happen when Peter went away?

"Our love will never disappear," Peter whispered in her ear, his lips grazing softly against her earlobe.

KC let her body fall against Peter as she enjoyed

the feel of his fluttery kisses.

"Hey, Josh," Winnie said, tapping him on the shoulder. "You see that?"

"See what?" Josh murmured, circling groups of numbers on his computer readouts with a red pencil.

"KC and Peter," Winnie said, tapping him again. "There's enough electricity between them to run the mainframe down at the computer center."

"What about the mainframe?" Josh asked, finally looking up.

Winnie collapsed on the grass, and her pink umbrella hat got crushed beneath her head. "Is that the only way I can get your attention?" she asked, taking off the hat and throwing it at Josh. "By talking computerspeak?"

"You always have my attention," Josh said, ignoring the hat and going back to work.

"Aaargh!" Winnie muttered, rolling back up into a sitting position. "What's happened to *our* passion, *our* romance?"

"Uh-huh," Josh said, circling another group of numbers.

KC was beginning to see Winnie's point. While it was clear Josh really cared about Winnie, he seemed more wrapped up in his work than his girlfriend.

"Floppy disk," Winnie said to Josh, reaching under his T-shirt to tickle his stomach.

Josh laughed and swatted Winnie's hand away.

"Megabyte!" Winnie teased, plucking a blade of overgrown grass and running it lightly down the bridge of his nose.

"Winnie!" Josh said in a patient voice. "I'm trying to study."

"Random access memory!" Winnie shouted, sweeping away Josh's papers and tackling him with a hug.

Josh lay there for a moment, calmly patting Winnie's back. Then, just as calmly, he lifted them both up, planted Winnie on the grass beside him, and picked up his papers again.

"You see how lucky you are, KC?" Winnie called to her. "You've got a man who really appreciates you."

Lucky? KC wanted to laugh. Even though Josh sometimes seemed distracted around Winnie, at least he was just a few yards down the hall. And he wasn't going anywhere. The two of them had months together, years, with no end in sight. But the end was looming for KC and Peter. Any day now, the news would come. And when it did, KC would ignore her own pain and just be happy for Peter.

She couldn't stand in his way. If letting him go was what it took to get Peter to accept the grant and go to Europe, then that's what she would do.

Her own feelings didn't matter.

"What are you thinking about?" Peter asked, wrapping one of KC's long brown curls around his index finger.

KC smiled. "I was just thinking about your glorious future, and how much you're going to learn in Europe."

"You have an active imagination," Peter said, enclosing her in his arms. "Remember, the odds are still against my winning this thing. I'm amazed I even made it to the finals. But believe me, that's as far as I'm going to get."

"How can you say that?" KC defended him. "I'll bet you're the most talented person who ever entered that contest. I'll bet the letter telling you you won is sitting in your mailbox right now."

"It's nice to have a fan club," Peter said, "but you'll see. I'm not going anywhere. I'll be hanging around this campus long after you've already gotten tired of me."

KC tried to laugh, but the beginning of a sob choked her. Didn't Peter realize that the idea of his staying on campus was just a fantasy? Peter was going to win that contest. There was no question about it.

The only question in KC's mind was how long it would be before they took Peter away from her.

Four
·····

*I*nhale, *two, three, four. Exhale, two, three, four.*

Melissa tried to use deep breathing techniques to clear her mind, to calm herself, but it didn't do any good. Her heart still beat faster than it did when she ran the 440. She still felt light-headed and the tightness in her chest remained. All she could think about was Brooks and her upcoming engagement party. She'd insisted on planning the whole thing, but she didn't have the slightest idea how to go about it.

She didn't have any money, and she certainly couldn't ask her parents since they had enough trouble putting food on their own table.

But letting the Baldwins treat them to dinner at Moreno's was out of the question. How could she let them arrange and pay for everything, while she and her penniless parents ate all that expensive food like a bunch of freeloaders?

"Think of this as a race," Melissa told herself. "Visualize yourself winning."

Melissa snickered at her own stupidity. There was no way she could win in this situation. It would be like racing against an Olympic track star. The Baldwins were yuppie types with graduate degrees, and nice clothes, and twin Saabs in the garage. Melissa's mother would probably show up in the same polka dot dress she wore to church every week, with the blue polyester blazer and fake flower corsage on the lapel. Melissa's father, if he even managed to get out of the house, would probably be unshaven and unwashed, his clothes hanging loosely off his skinny body.

Melissa could just picture the Baldwins' horrified faces when they saw the family their son was marrying into. Even though they'd liked Melissa when Brooks had brought her home to spend Thanksgiving with them, nothing could prepare them for the shock they were about to get. As soon as they met her parents, they'd probably demand

Brooks call off the wedding. And Melissa's parents would go into shock, too, since she hadn't even told them she was getting married in the first place.

"What a mess," Melissa groaned, covering her face with her pillow. She wanted to run away and hide, but then she realized she was already hiding, right here in her room.

"Knock, knock!" called a voice outside the door. It sounded like Faith, Brooks's ex-girlfriend.

Melissa stood up and checked her face in the mirror above her dresser. She didn't want Faith to see her falling apart. After all, Faith was still friends with Brooks, and Melissa couldn't risk having Brooks find out how panicky she was. Brooks would just insist on the original plan of his parents taking them out to dinner.

Inhale, two, three, four. Exhale, two, three, four. Melissa composed her face into a stiff mask, then opened the door.

"Am I too late?" Faith asked, rushing in, her head pivoting as she looked around the room. Her honey blond hair was twisted up in a large barrette, and she wore overall shorts over a sleeveless T-shirt. Faith turned to face Melissa. "I guess I missed everybody," she said.

"I'm sorry," Melissa said. "I don't know what you're talking about."

"That's okay," Faith said. "I was just supposed to meet Winnie, KC, and a bunch of other people to study, but I had to clean up all this drippy candle wax that Liza left all over our room. I can't believe her! I've told her lighting candles is a violation of dorm rules, but does she listen to me? Does she listen to anybody? No. She doesn't care that I'm on probation and can't afford another citation." Faith paused, looking embarrassed. "I'm sorry," she said. "I'm sure you don't want to hear my roommate troubles."

This was true. The last thing Melissa wanted was company, but she didn't want to seem rude. "No, please go on," Melissa said, trying to control her shaky voice. "It always helps to talk."

"Well, just shut me up if you get bored," Faith said, dropping down on Winnie's bed and taking a Japanese paper fan out of the netting above.

Melissa had never seen Faith so hyper. Usually, she was the mellow one who helped everyone else calm down. But today Faith seemed more super-charged than Winnie.

"I can't believe I've put up with Liza as long as I have," Faith ranted. "She's like the roommate from the black lagoon! As if the candle wax weren't bad enough, I was trying to get out of there so I could come over here, and she grabs my arm and starts babbling about how I have to make sure to come right back and go with her to the rec room lounge today at two o'clock to sign up for *Macbeth*. I told her it doesn't matter what time we sign up. The list will be up all week!"

"Hmmm," Melissa said as she sat down on her bed. She didn't trust her voice anymore. If she tried to talk, she might break down altogether.

"You know," Faith continued, fanning herself vigorously, "the more I think about it, the more I realize that it's Liza's fault my life is so screwed up right now. Liza's the one who introduced me to Scott. Liza's the one who figured out how to get me a fake ID, and Liza's the one who left me in the lurch at The Pub. . ."

Melissa nodded. Winnie had told her about Faith's run-in with campus security. But even though she felt sorry for Faith, she knew this was just a passing thing. Someday, she could put it all behind her.

Melissa's problems, on the other hand, would never go away. Brooks's parents and her parents would always be impossibly different from each other. Melissa's parents would always be poor, and her father would always be an alcoholic. Even if, by some miracle, she managed to throw an engagement party together, she'd just have to deal with these problems later on.

Melissa felt her lower lip quiver. She bit it to keep it from moving.

". . .and I just know she's going to get me another citation," Faith was raving. "Between her coffee pot, her candles, the posters she's tacked on the walls, and all the noise she makes . . ."

Melissa felt tears brimming in her eyes. *Please go away, Faith!* she silently begged. *I don't know how much longer I can keep this up!*

". . .and now, to top it all off, I have to put up with her parading around the room in her bathrobe as if she's Lady Macbeth." Faith threw down the fan and leaped off the bed, sticking her arms straight out in front of her as if she was holding something. *"While I stood rapt in the wonder of it, came missives from the King, who all-hailed me Thane of Cawdor."* Faith fell back onto Winnie's bed and picked up the fan again. "I swear, I know her whole speech by heart, I've heard it so many times."

Melissa's nose was starting to run now, and the tears were threatening to spill over any second.

"Well, I've talked your ears off," Faith said, tucking the fan back in the netting and getting up to leave. "Do you have any idea where Winnie and everybody else went?"

"No. . ." Melissa started to say, but the word

bubbled in her throat, and a tear leaked out of the corner of one eye.

"Melissa?" Faith asked. "Are you okay?"

It was too late. A sob erupted from deep inside her chest and tears started to stream down her face. "I'm sorry!" Melissa tried to say, but the words were lost in the guttural, wrenching cries that wracked her body. Melissa flung herself facedown on her bed and tried to smother the embarrassing sounds.

"Melissa!" Faith said, dropping to her knees beside the bed. "What's the matter?"

There was no point trying to hold back anymore. She probably couldn't even if she tried. So Melissa cried and cried, pounding her fists on the flimsy mattress. She cried until her nose was completely stuffed and her eyes were burning from the salty tears. She cried until she emptied herself out and lay exhausted, trying to breathe through her mouth. Faith, who had been stroking Melissa's hair, left the room and returned with a mug of cold water.

"Here," Faith said. "Drink something. You're probably dehydrated."

Melissa's throat was too swollen for her to say thank you, but she took the mug and let the water cool her throat. Then Faith got up again and brought a box of tissues over from Melissa's dresser.

"Blow your nose," Faith instructed, sitting on Winnie's bed and holding a tissue in front of Melissa's nose.

Melissa had to laugh, despite herself. Faith was making her feel like a little kid. But it was a nice feeling. Melissa knew Winnie jokingly referred to her as "Mother Faith," and now Melissa could see why.

"Tell me what's wrong," Faith said in that same no-nonsense, everything's-going-to-be-all-right tone.

Melissa sighed. How could she tell Faith? Nice as Faith was, she was still Brooks's ex-girlfriend. Not that it mattered, really. Faith had never acted jealous or possessive of Brooks. But Melissa didn't know her well enough to trust her. Come to think of it, she didn't trust *anybody* well enough to share her feelings.

"It's nothing," Melissa said, blowing her nose.

"Now why don't I believe you?" Faith asked.

"Well, it's nothing I can talk about," Melissa admitted. "It's too personal."

"Oh." Faith's brown eyes grew thoughtful. "Well, I don't want to pry."

"You're not prying," Melissa reassured her. "It's nice that you care enough to ask. It's just that it's so . . .embarrassing. I can't tell anybody."

"Whatever it is, you can't keep it in forever," Faith said. "It's going to burst out of you, one way or another. As you said, it really helps to talk to somebody."

Melissa nodded. "But if anyone finds out, if Brooks finds out. . ."

Melissa clasped a hand to her mouth. She'd almost given herself away. But Faith's expression stayed the same—calm, patient, understanding. It was so tempting just to tell her, just to see if she had any good advice. Besides, Faith knew Brooks better than anybody else. Maybe she would have some insight into his parents.

"If I tell you," Melissa said in a timid voice, "will you promise not to tell anybody else?"

Faith handed Melissa a clean tissue. "Of course!" she said. "I wouldn't have told anyone anyway. I never give away secrets."

Melissa nodded again and gritted her teeth. "I think I'm in over my head," she began. "Brooks sprang this engagement dinner on me without any warning, and I volunteered to take care of the whole thing even though I don't have the slightest idea how to go about it." When Melissa was done explaining her complicated situation, she grabbed her pillow and hugged it to her chest. "And now I don't know what to do," she concluded. "I can't back out of the dinner now, but I'm so afraid of what might happen when our parents meet."

"Why don't you talk it over with Brooks?" Faith suggested. "He won't let you deal with a problem all by yourself. He'll help you. He's really good that way."

"I know I should talk to him," Melissa said, blowing her nose again. "But I just can't."

"Why not?" Faith asked. "You're getting married. Couples are supposed to work things out together. That's what's supposed to make a good marriage."

"I want to be open with Brooks," Melissa said, "and I will be when we're married. But this isn't about openness. It's about my self-respect. I have to figure out a way to throw this party. If I let Brooks take over, I'll feel like some Fresh Air Fund kid with two charity cases for parents."

"It's all in your mind," Faith said. "Brooks doesn't see you that way. And neither does anybody else."

Faith's words were kind, but Melissa didn't really believe them. "Of course, I could just avoid the whole thing altogether if I don't tell my parents," she said, tossing her latest wadded tissue into the growing pile in the trash can.

"What?" Faith's eyebrows shot up. "Not tell them about the dinner? You can't do that."

"No. I mean tell them about the wedding."

Faith looked confused. Then her eyes grew very round and her mouth dropped open. "You mean you haven't told your parents you're getting married? You've been engaged for weeks!"

"I know," Melissa said, feeling her face grow hot. "I *want* to tell them. I just don't know how."

"How about a phone call?" Faith asked, bringing the tissue box over to Melissa and sitting beside her on the bed. "Or a visit. Don't they live right here in Springfield?"

"Getting in touch with them isn't the hard part," Melissa said, taking another tissue and dabbing at her still-running nose. "Facing them is. I wish I could just slip an anonymous note under their door telling them I'm engaged and giving them the time and the place for the party. That way if they want to show up, they can. And if they don't, I'm off the hook."

Faith's usually kind face hardened into a look of motherly disapproval, and Melissa felt even more like a little kid who'd gotten in trouble.

"I know," Melissa said. "I was only kidding. Sort of. I want them to come. It's just that . . ." Melissa felt her voice start to give way again. "I'm afraid . . ."

"Why?" Faith asked, her face full of concern. "What are you afraid of?"

"My dad . . . my dad's an alcoholic." Melissa's

voice cracked and more tears gathered in her eyes. "If someone offers him a drink . . . if he takes even one sip . . . he's a goner. He'll drink everything in sight and he won't stop 'til it's gone. Then he'll start getting mean and insulting people. Could you imagine how that would look to Brooks's parents? Why wasn't I born into some other family!" Melissa started to sob again.

"Oh, Melissa!" Faith comforted her. "I wish there was something I could do."

"Just don't tell anybody," Melissa pleaded.

Faith was silent for a moment.

"Faith?" Melissa asked, growing fearful. "You're not going to tell anyone, are you?"

"Well, no, not if you don't want me to. But I just had an idea. What if I went with you to your parents' house when you tell them you're engaged? It might be easier for you to tell them if I'm there— I'd be, like, a buffer zone."

Melissa looked at Faith in total disbelief. "You'd do that for me? You hardly know me!"

"I know you," Faith said. "You've been a good friend to Winnie. You make Brooks happy. I know you."

Melissa felt more tears well in her eyes, but these were tears of gratitude. "You're amazing, you know that?"

"I can help you with the dinner, too," Faith said. "We all can, if you're willing to let Winnie and KC in on this. Maybe we could find some place on campus to hold the dinner so it wouldn't cost much. And we could all cook something."

"No wonder Brooks was so in love with you," Melissa marveled. "You're a totally selfless person."

"Don't believe it," Faith said. "I just like to help people who deserve it. So, what do you think? Does it sound like a plan?"

Melissa couldn't believe how much things had changed in the past fifteen minutes. She'd gone from feeling desperate and alone to feeling maybe there was a little bit of hope. And she owed it all to Faith. It was weird teaming up with her fiancé's ex-girlfriend, but she already knew what her answer would be.

"Yes!" Melissa said, leaning forward to give Faith an awkward hug.

Five

"**W**hat have you gotten yourself into this time?" Faith asked herself as she left Melissa's room and headed down the stairs to the lobby of Forest Hall. Faith had been so caught up in Melissa's crisis that she'd offered to help without even thinking about how much work was involved. She was thinking about it now, though.

There was a menu to plan, groceries to buy, jobs to be assigned, and decorations to put up. She'd have to make a list for each general category so she wouldn't lose track of all the details. In fact, she'd have to make a list of all the lists she'd need before she could even get started.

But Faith wasn't sorry she'd volunteered. A big project like this engagement dinner was exactly what she needed to get back on track. Planning and organizing was what the old Faith did best, and Faith was determined to be that girl again. The girl who never got in trouble. The girl other people looked to for advice and comfort. The girl who could handle anything.

"Watch out!" a guy shouted as Faith reached the lobby. She ducked just in time to avoid being decapitated by a boomerang that whipped through the air, paused, then returned to the guy's outstretched hand.

"Sorry," the guy said, smiling foolishly. Faith glared. She'd come to expect this sort of thing from the jocks in Forest Hall. They considered the lobby and hallways of their dorm a linoleum-covered extension of the football field, the track, or the volleyball court.

Faith casually checked the lobby for the volleyball net that usually divided the room in two. Not that she was looking for Scott Sills, who could usually be found spiking volleyballs here when he wasn't at the gym. She'd barely thought about him at all since the time he'd apologized for leaving her alone in The Pub. She hadn't missed him or gone out of her way to run into him either.

It felt good to be in control of her life again. Now that she had her list of qualifications for Mr. Right, it would be easy to ignore anyone who didn't measure up.

Faith pushed open the lobby doors and was engulfed by ovenlike air as she started across the dorm green. The sun glared through a hazy wall of clouds, and the air was steamy. Faith was already sweating, and she hadn't been outside for more than a few seconds.

"Faith!"

Faith saw a pudgy figure come tottering across the green in spiky high heels, waving frantically.

"There you are!" Liza cried, stumbling as one of her heels sank into the grass. "I've been looking all over for you."

Liza looked as if she was dressed for the opera. She wore a fitted black velvet dress that came nearly to her ankles. Her curly reddish brown hair was gathered up in a bun, and she wore several long strands of fake pearls. Faith almost expected Liza to pull out a pair of long white gloves.

"Where are you going?" Faith asked.

"Don't tell me you don't remember!" Liza cried, grabbing Faith's arm. "We're late!"

"For what?"

"To sign up for the *Macbeth* auditions," Liza said, exasperated. "We were supposed to get to the rec center by two o'clock, and it's already five after."

"What's the big deal?" Faith asked as Liza dragged her down the hill toward the recreation center. "It's not first come, first served. Anyone who wants to can audition. And I'm not even trying out for a part. I just want to work on the stage crew."

"It's important to get there right away so we can be *seen*," Liza insisted. "Lawrence Briscoe might be there, so we have to make a good first impression."

"Is that why you're so dressed up?" Faith asked, beginning to lose feeling in her arm from Liza's pincerlike grip.

"I'm trying to look like a queen," Liza said in the same haughty voice she'd been using for Lady Macbeth. "I mean, I'm sure Briscoe has a wonderful imagination—did you see his production of *A Midsummer Night's Dream* on the educational channel?—but the right wardrobe can't hurt."

Liza's mouth kept moving, but Faith mentally turned down the volume. She'd gotten really good at that. It was the only way she could hear herself think. And right now she wanted to think about Melissa, not Liza.

Faith was still in shock at the intensity of Melissa's outburst. Faith had never suspected Melissa's fears and anxieties ran so deep. Until today, Melissa had always seemed so cool, so distant—so robotlike, actually. But maybe Melissa was more like a pressure cooker who'd kept the lid on too long.

Poor Melissa. She really did have a lot of family problems. But at least her love life was in order. She'd met her Mr. Right. And, knowing Brooks as well as she did, Faith knew that Melissa would always be loved and taken care of. It was more than Faith could be sure of herself, at this point.

"Well, here we are," Liza said, pulling Faith up the steps of a modern cement building right next to the dining commons. "I heard the sign-up sheet is in the lounge."

Faith couldn't even be sure of staying in school, at this rate. If Liza kept breaking dorm rules with her candles and her loud boom box, Faith would probably end up on the next bus back to Jacksonville.

But that was just negative thinking. Faith couldn't leave her fate up to Liza or Erin Grant. Faith was back in charge again, and Melissa's engagement dinner would prove it.

"You can let go of my arm now," Faith said, as Liza hauled her into the rec center. "I'm not going to run away."

Liza let go, leaving four white lines where her fingers had cut off the circulation in Faith's upper arm.

"Do I look okay?" Liza asked nervously, readjusting some of the hairpins in her bun.

Faith looked her over. Aside from being grossly overdressed, Liza didn't look too bad. With her new, more subdued hair color and lipstick, she looked better than Faith had ever seen her. Maybe if Liza got some encouragement, she'd tone herself down even further. "You look positively regal," Faith complimented her.

Liza grinned. "I hope Lawrence Briscoe thinks so."

The buzz of excited, chattering voices led Faith and Liza to the lounge. As soon as they entered the large room Faith realized that *she* was the one who hadn't dressed appropriately. Liza looked right at home among the elegantly coiffed young women, many of whom were wearing long black dresses like hers. Nearly all the guys wore jackets, also mostly black for that "artsy" look. Faith felt like a farmhand who'd wandered into the middle of a prom.

"So where is Lawrence Briscoe?" asked a tall, pretty girl who looked like a dancer. "I've been here since eleven o'clock this morning, just hoping to catch a glimpse of him."

"He's definitely on campus," answered a plump guy. "He arrived last night. But I doubt he'll make an appearance today. It would be beneath him."

"What do you mean?"

"Well, he's an internationally known director. He's not going to mingle with us common folk while we sign up. I'm sure we'll have to wait until the auditions before we see him."

"Where's he staying?" Liza asked, butting into the conversation.

Oh no, Faith thought. She could just imagine Liza barging in on Briscoe unannounced or, worse yet, climbing in his bedroom window, all the while reciting her letter speech from *Macbeth*.

"Nobody knows," said the plump young man. "I wish I did. I'd figure out some way to sneak in and do my speech from act two, scene one. *Is this a dagger which I see before me, the handle toward my hand?*"

Theater majors! They could be so pretentious, so self-centered. But at least Liza was involved in a conversation with someone else. This was Faith's chance to slip away. Now all she had to do was find the crew sheet, sign up for an interview with Briscoe, then make her getaway.

Well, at least there was one good thing about being here, Faith thought as she signed her name beneath dozens of others. It was all so comfortingly familiar. The gossip, the egos, the affected voices. It was exactly what Faith needed right now to make her feel her life was returning to normal.

Faith felt a tap on her shoulder. She turned,

expecting to see Meredith Paxton or Dante Borelli or one of her other theater friends. No doubt they wanted to brag about their latest starring role or report the latest sighting of Lawrence Briscoe.

But it wasn't a theater person. It was the last person she ever expected to see in a room full of well-dressed thespians. This person wore no jacket, no tie. In fact, he wore no shirt. He wasn't wearing any shoes, either. All he had on was a pair of baggy, tropical print swim trunks, and he carried an old leather helmet under his tan, muscular arm.

"Scott!" Faith stammered. "What are you doing here?"

Scott didn't answer right away. He looked just as embarrassed as Faith felt. His shaggy blond hair was bleached pale by the sun, and his face looked just as healthy and sincere as ever. It was hard to believe that this adorable guy was the same person who'd abandoned her when she was in trouble.

"What am I doing here?" Scott echoed, his amber eyes flitting about the room. "You know, it's funny, I was asking myself the same thing. I was looking for my touch football game, but I guess I took a wrong turn. Why are these people wearing so many clothes? Don't they know it's ninety degrees outside?"

Faith felt a smile start to twitch the corners of her mouth, but she fought it. "I'm sure they'd be more comfortable if they dressed like you. But your head might get hot in that helmet. That *is* a helmet, isn't it? I thought they didn't make them like that anymore."

"My friend Larry gave it to me as a joke. It belonged to his grandfather. Larry said some of his grandfather's brain waves were still in the helmet. If I wear it, my game might improve."

"Oh, I see," Faith said, feeling her lips twitch again. "You're supposed to absorb the brain waves by osmosis."

"Exactly!"

Scott grinned, and Faith felt herself melt, just a little. He seemed so harmless, like an innocent little kid who just wanted to play and have a good time. But that, Faith reminded herself, was the sort of attitude that had gotten her in trouble before. She wasn't a little kid. She was a responsible adult. Still, she'd said she'd give him another chance.

"So how's the volleyball going?" Faith asked, allowing the twitch to form a small smile.

"Great!" Scott said. "We're going to the state finals next week. If we win, we'll move on to the regionals."

"What's the winning streak up to now?" Faith asked. "Twenty in a row?"

"Twenty-one," Scott said. "It's a new record. I'm going to be in the history books!"

"Pretty impressive."

"Yeah . . ." Scott's eyes flitted around the room again. "So, why is everybody wearing black? Did somebody die?"

Faith laughed before she remembered not to. "No. They're signing up to audition for *Macbeth* or work on the crew. There's a famous director directing it, and I think people were expecting to see him today."

"Oh, I get it," Scott said, nodding his shaggy head. "Dressing like you're going to a funeral makes you look more sophisticated, right?"

Faith looked at Scott in appreciation. He was probably the only person in the room who saw things the way she did. But of course, they only saw eye to eye in this one tiny area. In every other way, they were incompatible.

He was wild and uninhibited.

She was practical and steady.

He had no goals in life, other than to enjoy himself.

She was planning to work hard and make a name for herself in the theater.

Besides, he hadn't done anything to make up for leaving her alone at The Pub. She had no reason to trust him.

"So . . . " Scott said, shoving his hands in the pockets of his swim shorts. "I guess you're going to be pretty busy working on this play, huh?"

Faith could see where this was going, but she wasn't sure how to answer. "Well, they're just starting to gear up," Faith said. "The actual work won't start for at least another week."

Scott glanced briefly at Faith's face, then down at the floor. "Does that mean you'll have some free time? To go out with me, I mean."

He looked so sad, and his skin looked so soft. Faith had a sudden urge to touch the muscles of his bare arms. But that was simply physical attraction, which had nothing to do with common sense.

"I'm sorry," Faith said. "But I'm still going to be really busy. I'm planning a big engagement dinner for a friend of mine, and there are so many details to think about. It's a week from Sunday, and I haven't even figured out the menu yet."

"I could help you," Scott offered. "I worked at a couple of different restaurants when I was in high school. I was a waiter, a salad man, a busboy. I could give you *professional* advice. For a small fee, of course." Scott grinned, and Faith found herself grinning back.

"How much?" she asked.

"It's all in the contract," Scott said. "Just don't read the fine print."

Faith was tempted. Compared to these nervous,

showy theater majors, Scott was a breath of fresh air. On the other hand, how could she take him seriously when he walked around half-dressed? No one else seemed to take him seriously, either. People kept staring at him and whispering.

"What part are *you* trying out for?" asked a throaty female voice. "I didn't know they had beach bums in Elizabethan times."

Faith turned. Erin Grant had appeared from the crowd. Her long black hair hung to her waist, and her makeup had been carefully applied to emphasize the icy blue of her eyes. She wore a black dress with a handkerchief hemline. No doubt Erin was hoping to win the part of Lady Macbeth, but to Faith, she looked more like one of the three witches.

Erin was staring at Scott with disdain. "By the way, are you aware that there's a university regulation requiring all students to wear both shirts *and* shoes in all public places on campus?"

Scott shrugged. "Sorry."

"Just be glad I'm not your R.A.," Erin said. With a nasty smile at Faith, she walked away.

"I wish she wasn't *my* R.A.," Faith said, watching Erin add her name to the sign-up sheet. "As long as I'm on probation, she's got the power of life and death over me."

Scott shuddered. "I wouldn't want someone like

that breathing down my neck. She's got cold eyes."

"I'm trying not to think about her," Faith said, "but she asked a good question. What *are* you doing here, Scott? And don't give me that line about taking a wrong turn."

Scott looked surprised. "Why do you think? I came to see you, of course!"

"But how did you know I'd be here?"

"Liza told me."

"Liza?"

Scott nodded. "I kept waiting to bump into you by accident, but it never happened, so I finally went by your room the other day. Your roommate told me you'd be here at two o'clock."

Faith pressed her lips together and fumed. So that was why Liza had been so insistent that they show up here precisely at two o'clock. What did Faith have to do to get that girl to mind her own business—tie her up with ropes and stuff her in a closet? The idea was very tempting.

And how like Scott to just drift for the past two weeks, waiting for fate to bring them together, rather than just call her on the phone like a normal person and arrange a date. Did he think Faith was going to keep her feelings on hold until he got around to showing up? How presumptuous!

"Sorry, Scott," Faith said, "but arranging an accident is hardly the way to impress me. I don't need any more accidents in my life right now. I like to know in advance when I'm going to see someone. And I like knowing when someone's going to disappear. I'll never have that with you."

Scott's face fell and, for a moment, he didn't say anything. Then he sighed. "Okay," he said. "I don't want to force you into anything. But if you change your mind and want to see me again, give me a call. I'll leave it up to you."

"Bye, Scott," Faith said.

Without another word, Scott padded out of the lounge, the muscles of his broad back highlighted by the recessed lighting up in the ceiling.

Faith sank into the cushions of the red seating unit and closed her eyes. Why did she feel so sad? Scott wasn't her Mr. Right. He was only half-Right. She didn't even feel comfortable asking him to help her at Melissa's engagement party. He probably wouldn't show up in the first place. Actually, it would be better if he didn't show up—he was the last person Melissa needed if she wanted an uneventful, *sober* party.

This whole thing was Liza's fault. Every bit of it. Ever since she'd bought Lauren's dorm contract, Liza had been like a splinter under Faith's skin. Everything about her was so annoying. Her brassy voice, her horsey laugh, the cheap, fruity smell of her perfume. Her shrine of self-portraits hanging above her bed.

How had Faith come to this? Her life had been so calm and predictable when she'd had Lauren for a roommate and Brooks for a boyfriend. But those days were gone forever.

Six

....

Early Saturday afternoon, Winnie threw herself over the front seat of the car so she could turn up the air conditioner. After six days in a row of ninety-degree temperatures, she was beginning to feel as if her clothes were permanently plastered to her skin. She paused for a moment, her hips balanced over the back of the seat, so that the frigid air could cool her sweaty face.

"Lock your doors, everybody," Melissa warned as Faith drove them through the streets of Springfield.

Winnie, teetering between her old friend and her roommate, looked out the window. Sure there were a few vacant lots and a burned-out tenement or two, but the area wasn't that bad. Some of the blocks they'd passed had rows of neat, if slightly shabby, brownstones, or low-rise apartment buildings with flower boxes in the windows.

"This was a really crummy idea," Melissa said, looking uncomfortable in a navy linen suit. The suit had already gotten horribly wrinkled in the five minutes they'd been in the car, and the white blouse she wore underneath was moist with sweat. "You guys don't have to come home with me. Why don't we just go back to campus, and I'll break the news to my parents some other way."

They were on their way to Melissa's parents' house, in downtown Springfield. After weeks of putting it off, Melissa was finally going to tell her parents that she was engaged and invite them to the engagement dinner next Sunday. It was about time, too. Melissa had delayed so long, Winnie was beginning to wonder if she'd ever tell them.

Winnie just couldn't understand it. If she had news like this, she'd tell everybody she knew. She'd even stop people on the street. She'd dance around and make up her own silly version of "I'm Getting Married in the Morning."

Not that she was ready to get married, yet. But she'd be so happy that something exciting had happened to her, something romantic, something *different*. The way things were going with Josh right now, it looked as if she'd never feel excited about their relationship again. Sure, she still loved him, and he loved her. But there were no sparks anymore, just a calm sameness and a taking for granted.

"Sorry, Melissa," Faith said, carefully steering around a homeless man. "You're not getting rid of us that easily."

"That's right," Winnie said, turning up the air conditioner a notch. "When we give moral support, you can't give it back."

"You know, I really *can* face my parents alone," Melissa said as they passed an overturned, stripped car at the side of the road. "There's nothing to be scared of. They may be my parents, but they're just people. And getting married's not a crime. I'm eighteen. Legally, I'm entitled to do whatever I want."

Winnie noticed that Melissa was having trouble breathing. Actually, she wasn't so much breathing as sighing. One sigh after another. And she kept touching her fingertips to her chest as if she were in pain.

"So, have you figured out what you're going to say to your parents?" Winnie asked Melissa, as Faith slowed down for a stop sign.

"I don't know why I have to say anything at all," Melissa muttered, touching her fingers to her chest again. "It's my life. Not theirs."

Melissa was just like some of Winnie's callers at the Crisis Hot Line. People would call because they were in serious trouble, yet they still denied it. Winnie sometimes had to work harder convincing them they had a problem than she did *solving* the problem.

Maybe that was the way to get through to Melissa. But Winnie couldn't lay it on too thick, or Melissa might shut down completely. Melissa hated feeling vulnerable. A lighter approach was more in order.

"You know, you're right," Winnie said. "You don't need us. You don't even need to go yourself. There are plenty of other ways to get a message across."

Faith took her eyes off the road for a second and gave Winnie a questioning look.

"Sure!" Winnie said, placing a slightly sticky arm around Melissa's shoulder. "With today's technology, there are so many means of communication. Like skywriting. Smoke signals. Carrier pigeons."

"Very funny, Win," Melissa said.

"I'm sure your parents don't want to see you, anyway," Winnie added. "I mean, when was the last time you got together? Christmas? They're probably sick of you by now."

"I know I should visit them more . . ." Melissa began.

"Don't be silly!" Winnie said. "They live much too far away. What is it, two miles from campus?

That's at least a twenty-minute walk. Or a ten-minute run, at your speed."

"Okay! Okay!" Melissa said, covering her hands with her ears. "I admit it. I've been avoiding them. I'm scared to death. I don't have the first idea what to say to them. There. You satisfied?"

Winnie smiled. "Of course not," Winnie said. "I won't be satisfied until we come up with a solution."

"How about this?" Melissa asked. "'Hi, Mom. Hi, Dad. I'm getting married. Good-bye.'"

"Brief, yet to the point," Winnie said. "But it's important to let them know you care about how they feel so they'll be more receptive to what you say. Like, how about saying, 'Hi, Mom. Hi, Dad. *How are you?* I'm getting married. Good-bye.'"

The neat row houses gave way to tiny single family homes, mostly clapboard, some with sagging front porches. A few had scraggly bushes and patches of green in the yards, but most were surrounded by concrete.

"I think the *first* thing you should do is give them both a big hug and a kiss," Faith said as she paused at another stop sign, then continued across the intersection. "Warm up to the real topic gradually. Start talking about school, casually mention that you've met a wonderful guy, tell them a little bit about Brooks, *then* break the news. At least that way they won't be totally shocked."

"It won't matter," Melissa said, turning her head and staring out the window. Damp wisps of her copper-colored hair stuck to the back of her neck. "They're going to be shocked no matter how I bring it up. That is, if my father isn't already in a stupor. Let's see, what time is it? One o'clock. He should have had a couple of six packs by now. I'd be surprised if he remembers my name."

"He'll remember," Faith said. "And then you should invite them to the engagement dinner. Tell them how much Brooks's parents are looking forward to meeting them."

Melissa's whole body went rigid. "This dinner's going to be a total disaster. I can feel it."

"It is not," Faith insisted. "It's going to be great. I've already figured out the whole thing."

"Yeah," Winnie said. "Have faith in Faith."

"I'm sorry," Melissa said, trying to pull out some of the creases in her skirt. "I didn't mean to sound ungrateful. So what have you figured out?"

"Well," Faith went on, "as I was leaving the *Macbeth* sign-ups Thursday, I noticed a really nice reception room in the rec center. It had wall-to-wall carpet and recessed lighting and a big table. I'm going to find out if we can reserve it for the dinner."

Melissa forced a smile. "Good thinking."

"I had some other thoughts about the food, too," Faith said, "if you don't mind a few other people getting involved."

"How many?" Melissa asked.

"Well, uh, just a couple. Me, KC, Winnie, Josh, Peter, Brooks's roommate Barney Sharfenburger, Kimberly, Derek, and Lauren."

"That's half the school!" Melissa sputtered. "Why would all those people want to help me?"

"Believe me, Melissa, they do," Winnie put in. "They *like* you!"

"It would be like our engagement present to you," Faith said. "We'd do all the shopping, cooking, decorations, and cleanup. We could even assign someone to keep an eye on your father to make sure he doesn't drink. That way you won't have to worry he'll go overboard."

Melissa stared out the window and didn't say anything.

"What's wrong?" Winnie asked.

"It's too much," Melissa said in a gruff voice. "I can't ask people to do all that for me."

"You don't have to ask," Faith said. "We volunteered."

"I'm sorry," Melissa said, sitting up tall and straightening out her jacket. "I can't let you."

Why did Melissa have to put up such a fight every

time someone wanted to do something nice for her? Pride was one thing, but now she was just being perverse. Or maybe she was just trying to prove she had a stronger will than anybody else. No matter what it was, Winnie wasn't going to let her get away with it. Melissa might not realize she deserved this, but Winnie did.

"Try and stop us!" Winnie challenged her room-mate.

"Let's put it this way," Faith said. "Dinner will be on the table at six o'clock a week from today. So you can either show up or not. It's up to you."

"But you wouldn't let all that good food go to waste, would you?" Winnie asked, leaning forward to catch Melissa's eye.

Melissa sighed and shook her head. "I know when I've been double-teamed. Okay, you guys. If you're really sure you want to do this, then I'm very grateful for your help."

"Good," Faith said, tapping the steering wheel. "I'll work things out in a little more detail, then I'll meet with you and Brooks early next week to go over everything."

"Uh-oh," Melissa said, slumping in her seat.

"What?" Winnie asked. "Did you change your mind again?"

"No," Melissa said, her chin grazing the gold buttons on her jacket. "We're here."

"We are?" Faith asked, putting on the brakes. "Which house?"

Melissa nodded toward a delapidated one-story house on the right side of the street.

Though Winnie knew Melissa's family was poor, she hadn't expected the house to look this bad. It was clapboard like the others, with peeling white paint, broken window shutters, and a front screen door that hung at a crazy angle. There were a few overgrown weeds in the front yard, but that was the only sign of life.

"Looks like no one's home," Winnie said, trying not to let her surprise show on her face. "There's no car in the driveway."

"We don't have a car," Melissa mumbled as Faith pulled up in front of the house.

"Oh," Winnie said. "Sorry."

"It's not your fault," Melissa said as Faith put the car in "Park" and turned off the engine. "It's not your fault no one in my family cares that they live in a rathole. It's not your fault my brother looks like a reject from a heavy metal concert. It's not your fault my father's sat in the same chair for eight years without changing his clothes."

"Calm down, Melissa," Faith said. "If you're worried about what we'll think of your family, don't.

I'm sure they're very nice people."

"Nice!" Melissa yelled. "They're not going to seem nice when they find out about the engagement. My mother's going to scream bloody murder. You'll see."

"She won't," Winnie assured her. "Come on. Let's get out of the car."

Melissa sank so far down in her seat that the top of her head was lower than the window. "I can't."

"But how will they find out you're engaged?" Winnie asked. "And how will they know about the dinner?"

Melissa crossed her arms over her chest and pressed her lips together.

Winnie had never seen Melissa act so childish and stubborn. There was only one thing to do—outwit her again with reverse psychology.

"Fine," Winnie said. "Then *I'll* tell them." She glanced down at Melissa, hoping her words would scare Melissa into sitting up and getting out of the car. Melissa couldn't want a stranger to break news like that to her parents.

"Fine," Melissa said. "*You* tell them."

Winnie gulped. She wasn't exactly prepared for this. But if this was the only way the McDormands were going to find out, then it had to be done. Winnie sat down on the backseat and shoved her feet into her already-tied running shoes.

"I'll go with you," Faith said, opening her door.

"Last chance, Melissa," Winnie said, her hand poised on the door handle.

"Have fun," Melissa said dourly.

Winnie got out of the car and slammed the door behind her. Maybe once Melissa saw they were serious, she'd come to her senses. But all Melissa did was shift up slightly in her seat so she could watch Winnie and Faith head up the short cement walk.

"What do we do now?" Winnie asked, beginning to panic.

"Break it to them as gently as possible," Faith said, straightening the hem of her flowered sun dress.

Winnie felt her heart skitter inside her chest, but there was no turning back now. Besides, they were already on the front doostep. Winnie pressed the doorbell.

A moment later, the front door opened inward. Standing behind the tilting screen door was an overweight, middle-aged woman. Her brown hair was mixed with gray, and her face looked jowly and tired. She wore a sleeveless blue-and-white striped shirt, untucked, over a brown plaid skirt, and a pair of rubber flip-flops. Winnie studied the woman closely, but she didn't see even a hint of resemblance to Melissa.

"Yes?" the woman asked.

"Mrs. McDormand?" Winnie asked.

"Yes."

"I'm Winnie Gottlieb. Melissa's roommate. And this is my friend Faith Crowley."

"Is something wrong?" Mrs. McDormand asked, her tired face coming alive with anxiety.

"No, nothing," Winnie quickly assured her, pointing toward the car. "Melissa's back there."

Mrs. McDormand looked over Winnie's shoulder, and her face relaxed back into tiredness. "She doesn't want to come in?"

"She's a little . . . nervous," Faith said. "She has some big news . . . wonderful news, really . . . but she wasn't sure how you'd take it."

"So she sent you two to tell me?"

"Something like that," Winnie said.

"I'd invite you in," Mrs. McDormand said, "but my husband isn't feeling too well this afternoon. He's napping in the living room."

"That's fine," Faith assured her. "We won't take too much of your time."

"So?" Mrs. McDormand asked. "What's the news?"

Faith looked a little scared, so Winnie decided to jump right in. "Melissa's been dating a really nice guy," Winnie said. "His name is Brooks Baldwin, and we both grew up with him, so if you have any questions about his family or his childhood, we're the right people to ask. He was the smartest kid in my nursery school class, even though he wasn't too good about taking naps, but he always got good marks in sharing and snacktime."

Faith tugged on Winnie's arm and cupped a hand to her ear. "I don't think you need to go quite that far back," she whispered.

Winnie smiled sheepishly. "Sorry. I just meant that Brooks is a good guy."

"He's really serious and ambitious," Faith offered. "Good looking, athletic . . . "

"Very stable and dependable," Winnie added, knowing that these were qualities that appealed to parents.

"That's nice," Mrs. McDormand said.

"Well, that's not quite the whole thing," Winnie said. She took a deep breath and forced the words out of her mouth. "Melissa and Brooks are engaged."

Mrs. McDormand's eyebrows shot up. Winnie waited for the bloody screams Melissa had promised, but Mrs. McDormand didn't say anything.

"I know it's kind of a shock," Winnie said. "I mean, I know how I'd feel if *my* daughter got engaged so young, but—"

A quick poke from Faith ended that line of

reasoning. Winnie felt bad for even bringing up a sore point.

"Please give Melissa my congratulations," Mrs. McDormand said, with some grace. "Tell her Dad and I wish her the best of luck."

Winnie felt a lump appear in her throat. Was this the woman Melissa had been so afraid of facing? This woman had real dignity, despite her rundown house and shabby clothes.

"You can tell her yourself," Faith said. "Next Sunday at six o'clock we're throwing an engagement dinner for your family and the Baldwins at the campus rec center."

"We really hope you can come," Winnie added.

Mrs. McDormand looked behind her, as if consulting with someone Winnie couldn't see. Winnie wondered if Mr. McDormand was sitting there in the living room, in his usual chair the way Melissa had described him, and if he'd heard their conversation by the door. Or maybe he was passed out and Mrs. McDormand was just looking at him while she made up her mind.

Mrs. McDormand turned back to Winnie and looked at her with tired eyes. "We don't have any other plans. We'll be happy to come."

"Great!" Winnie said, breathing a huge sigh of relief. This hadn't been nearly as difficult as she'd thought.

"But please tell Melissa this," Mrs. McDormand said, looking once again over Winnie's shoulder at her sulking daughter in the car. "Tell Melissa I hope she knows what she's getting into. I'm sure she's all caught up in the excitement of being in love right now, but that excitement fades quickly. And when it does, you never know if there's going to be anything there."

Winnie nodded seriously. "I'll tell her."

"It's easy to be infatuated," Mrs. McDormand went on, "but marriage is a totally different story. You've got to be willing to make a lifetime commitment, to stick with someone no matter how bad things get. You've got to be willing to compromise. It's a lot of hard work. And I don't know if Melissa's really ready for that."

Melissa wasn't going to be happy to hear any of this, but Winnie had given her word. Or maybe Faith could tell her.

"Thank you for coming, girls," Mrs. McDormand said, starting to close the front door. "We'll see you next Sunday."

As Winnie trudged back toward Kimberly's car, Mrs. McDormand's words kept repeating themselves over and over. *The excitement fades quickly. Compromise. Hard work.* Those words sounded awfully familiar. But they didn't have anything to do with Melissa.

Words like that had been echoing through Winnie's brain a lot lately. Because words like that perfectly described the way her relationship was going with Josh right now. Compared to the fire and excitement between Peter and KC, Winnie and Josh were like an old married couple. Maybe their first stage of infatuation was over.

But could that be? So soon? They were still so young. And if they ended up together, did that mean that Winnie would never feel a romantic thrill again? Never feel that burst of adrenaline when a guy walked in the room? Never see that look of desire in his eyes?

Winnie had always lived for that kind of excitement. She'd thrived on it. The thought of spending the rest of her life without it was a very scary notion.

While Winnie and Faith were getting back in Kimberly's car, KC was standing on the sidewalk in front of the Tri Beta sorority house, waiting for Peter to pick her up.

How many more? a little voice in her head asked. *How many more dates with Peter before you say goodbye?*

KC tried to find another voice inside her to argue the other side of the issue. Maybe they'd never have to say good-bye. Peter hadn't heard a word yet on the Morgan Foundation grant. Maybe that meant he wasn't going to win.

But there wasn't any voice to make that argument, because no part of her believed it. The days were passing quickly. Any day now, the letter would be waiting in Peter's mailbox. The letter that would tell them how few days they had left together.

The distant whine of an engine sounded as sweet to KC's ears as *I love you*, because it was the sound of Peter's motorcycle, bringing him closer and closer. As KC watched Peter zip down Greek Row, she tried to memorize this feeling, too—the feeling of Peter coming, not going.

Peter screeched to a stop in front of KC and whipped off his helmet. "Excuse me, Miss," he said with a nasal twang, "but I'm from out of town and I'm looking for the Tri Beta museum. I hear they have the world's largest collection of pink lace doilies. I couldn't pass through Springfield without seeing that."

"Peter!" KC cried, playfully slapping his arm. Peter was always making fun of sororities, and even though KC had spent months trying to get into Tri Beta, the most exclusive sorority on campus, she didn't take his teasing as seriously as she used to.

Peter grabbed KC and lifted her onto the broad

leather seat of his motorcycle so that she was sitting sidesaddle. KC loved the way he could lift her so easily. It made her feel light as air, and very safe and protected.

"How was your meeting?" Peter asked, wrapping his arms around her.

"Unh-unh." KC shook her head and pointed to her lips. "Kiss first. Information later."

Peter pretended to look torn. "Gee, I don't know. A whole kiss? Both lips? It sounds like a pretty steep price to pay. But that's what I get for negotiating with a sharp businesswoman like you."

"Pay up. Now," KC demanded.

Peter grabbed KC and kissed her hungrily, tilting her head back. KC responded with her whole body, grabbing his bare arms, running her fingers up and down his back, stroking his silky hair. Finally, reluctantly, they broke apart, and KC felt a lump rise in her throat.

How many more? the voice demanded. *How many more kisses?*

"Hop on!" Peter invited her.

KC climbed on the motorcycle behind Peter, glad she'd worn bicycle shorts beneath her pleated cotton skirt.

"So have you figured out where you want to go?" Peter asked. "You want to drive up to the mountains? Or go to Hosmer Lake? It's a lot cooler up there."

"Let's go to Coleridge first," KC said, steeling herself as she had every day this week.

"Now?" Peter asked. "Why don't we wait 'til we get back?"

KC wrapped her arms around Peter's waist and leaned her head against the back of his shoulder. "I have to know," she whispered. "If the letter from the Morgan Foundation is in the mailbox, I have to face up to it. You've got to be curious, too."

Peter nodded. "Okay." He handed KC her helmet and put on his, and the two rode in silence to Coleridge Hall. As Peter parked his motorcycle a few moments later, KC's heart began to pound. This could be it—the moment she'd been dreading. They'd said the letter would arrive this week, and this was Saturday, the last day of the week.

Holding hands, KC and Peter entered the building and took the stairs down to the basement, where the mailboxes were. KC clung to Peter as they walked together down the empty linoleum corridor between the brass boxes. She could feel his strong pulse, beating in synch with her own.

At last they reached Peter's mailbox, and he knelt down to unlock it. Peter reached in his hand, and they both froze as he withdrew it. In it was a single beige envelope with an embossed logo for the return address. KC didn't even need to look at the filigreed *M* to know exactly what it was.

Peter just stared at the envelope from the Morgan Foundation as if afraid to open it.

"Go ahead," KC said softly, her hands clenched into fists. "You deserve to know their decision."

Peter looked up at KC, his hazel eyes eager and afraid and miserable all at the same time. He continued looking at her as he ran his finger under the flap of the envelope and ripped it open. Then, tearing his eyes away from KC, he removed the letter and read it quickly.

KC agonized as she searched his face for clues, but he betrayed no emotion whatsoever. "Tell me!" she begged. "I can't take it anymore!"

Silently, Peter handed the letter to KC. Forcing her eyes to skim the first few lines, she felt her whole body go limp. The waiting was over.

Dear Mr. Dvorsky,
On behalf of the Morgan Foundation, I am very pleased to offer you my congratulations. After reviewing the portfolios of over one thousand applicants in the "Portrait" category, we have selected you as the recipient of the grand prize: a year's photography study in Florence and a four-page feature spread in Photography *magazine. We will be in touch with you soon regarding*

*travel and accommodations. Meanwhile, our
heartfelt good wishes.*

> *Very truly yours,*
> *Nicholas Calanni, Director*

KC felt a chill wash over her. Peter had won.

For a moment, KC and Peter simply stared at each other without speaking or moving. It was a new beginning for Peter, but it was also an ending. Things between them would never be the same.

KC finally threw her arms around Peter and hugged him as tight as she could. "I'm so happy for you," she sobbed, tears bursting from her eyes. "And I love you so much!"

"I love you, too," Peter answered in a choked voice.

"This is so great," KC insisted, careless of the tears splashing down on Peter's shoulder. "You're going to be really rich and famous someday. And it all started here."

"I know," Peter said, his own tears falling into KC's hair. "It's a wonderful thing."

"Just wonderful," KC echoed, before she lost the ability to speak altogether.

Seven

"*Glamis thou art, and Cawdor, and shalt be what thou art promised . . .*" Liza muttered under her breath as she sat in the airless lounge of the rec center, waiting to be called for her audition with Lawrence Briscoe. Half a dozen of the competition were scattered around the lounge, also waiting.

Though Liza recognized every one of these girls from the theater department, they each sat separately, mouthing lines, staring into space, or giving each other jealous, appraising looks. Liza ignored them all. There really wasn't any competition, anyway. She was the only one who mattered.

Liza could hardly believe that she'd actually be meeting the great Briscoe in person, in just a few minutes. She'd scoured the campus since last Thursday, hoping for a glimpse of him, but he'd been laying pretty low. No one had seen him.

"Yet I do fear thy nature . . ."

There was no point in going over her lines again. She'd memorized her monologue over a week ago and had repeated it a hundred times a day since then, as Faith kept reminding her.

Liza would have thought Faith would be grateful she'd arranged for Scott to see her last week, but Faith hadn't said a word about it. And today, as Liza was getting dressed for her audition, Faith had blown up at her just because she'd lit a few candles and had gotten a teeny bit of wax on one of Faith's notebooks. Didn't Faith have any perspective at all? What was a little bit of wax when Liza was about to leave for the most important audition of her life? Liza had offered to clean it up later, but that wasn't good enough for Faith. Faith had stood there and screamed until Liza had thrown every candle in the garbage can.

Liza had obeyed, even though it had almost made her late for her audition. Liza still wanted to prove to her roommate that she was a worthwhile person, someone Faith should want to be friends with. But if she didn't prove it by cleaning up the candles, she was going to prove it soon, when she read for Briscoe.

Not that Faith deserved all the time Liza spent thinking about her. Faith hadn't even invited Liza to the engagement dinner she was planning for Melissa and Brooks. Faith had invited everyone else she knew. And all the people she'd invited were Liza's friends, too. Or, at least, they used to be. But now it seemed as if Faith was turning KC, Winnie, and Lauren against her.

Why did Faith hate her so much? Liza had done nothing but nice things for her. Yet, once again, Liza had ended up feeling left out and alone. Liza was beginning to think she'd feel this way for the rest of her life.

Now Liza was angry that she'd wasted these valuable last few minutes before her audition worrying about Faith. Who needed friends, anyway, when you could have stardom? She'd have plenty of hangers-on, once she was famous. That was almost as good.

"Liza Ruff?"

Liza recognized the guy in the doorway who'd called her name. It was Meredith Paxton, a junior from the drama department who stage-managed a lot of the shows.

Liza stood up and smoothed her dress. "Ready," she told Meredith.

As Liza followed Meredith's rumpled back down the hall, she tried not to think about the fact that Lawrence Briscoe had been interviewed by Johnny Carson, David Letterman, and Arsenio Hall. She tried not to think about the fact that, though he was only twenty-nine years old, he'd already directed some of the most distinguished Shakespearean actors in Great Britain. Liza tried not to think about the fact that she was just a college freshman trying out for a school production. Once she got inside, they'd be equals—two artists working for a common goal.

Who was she kidding? She was terrified.

Meredith opened the door to a large office and poked his head inside. "Liza Ruff," he said, making a check on the clipboard he was carrying.

Feeling as if she were going to faint against the doorjamb, Liza forced herself to take a deep breath. Then she put on her most dazzling smile and marched into the room.

A young man sat behind an antique mahogany desk lit by a brass banker's lamp with a green shade. He wore a black turtleneck, despite the heat, and a black blazer with broad shoulders. He wasn't exactly handsome, but there was something compelling about him. Maybe it was the precise way his brown hair was slicked straight back from his high fore-head. Maybe it was his glowering eyes beneath the thick brows, or his gaunt cheekbones.

He rose from the table, revealing more height than Liza had been expecting, and came around the desk, meeting Liza on the thick Oriental rug that took up most of the floor. Against the side wall, beneath a window with closed venetian blinds, was an oversized black leather sofa with thick cushions. Liza wondered if the university had made the room so cosy just for the visiting director, but then she noticed a diploma on the wall with the name of a professor who was on sabbatical.

The young man extended his hand. Liza noticed that his fingers were long and delicate. "Lawrence Briscoe," he said, his British accent as impeccable as his hair.

Liza shook his hand vigorously, still finding it hard to believe that he was really flesh and blood. "Liza Ruff," she said. "I'm absolutely thrilled to meet you."

Briscoe smiled warmly. "And I'm equally thrilled to meet such an attractive young woman. That's a lovely dress you're wearing."

Liza couldn't believe what she was hearing. This famous, striking, talented director actually thought she was attractive! Talk about starting an audition on the right foot.

"Thank you," Liza said, self-consciously smoothing the brand new burgundy dress she'd bought especially for this audition.

"So what have you prepared?" Briscoe asked, his intense eyes seeming to absorb her all at once.

"The letter scene," Liza said.

"Very good." Briscoe perched himself on the edge of the desk, just a few feet from Liza. "Whenever you're ready."

Ready? Liza had been ready all her life. And this was the moment to prove it. Liza closed her eyes, trying to conjure up the image of Macbeth's castle she'd carried with her for the past week. She tried to think about the candles she'd kept burning, to provide the atmosphere of evil, fear, and decay. But candles just brought back all the anger and resentment she was feeling toward Faith.

She could use that, though. Lady Macbeth was seething, herself, with ambition and desire and rage.

"They met me in the day of success; and I have learned by the perfect's report they have more in them than mortal knowledge . . ." Liza began, pantomiming the letter just sent her by her husband, Macbeth.

As Liza continued to read of Macbeth's ambition for the throne, she felt the surging and boiling of her own ambition. Her desire for fame, for applause, for greatness, it was no different from the emotions of Lady Macbeth. Soon, Liza stopped noticing any division between herself and her character. They were one. One big bubbling cauldron of "I Want."

It took Liza a few seconds, in the silence that followed her reading, to remember where she was or even *who* she was. Then it all came back to her. Liza hastily glanced over at Lawrence Briscoe, who gazed at her intently.

"Hmmmm . . . " was all he said.

Liza wasn't sure what to do. Briscoe undoubtedly was a very busy man. Maybe "Hmmm" was all she was going to get. Liza backed up a step, toward the door.

"Let's chat," Briscoe suddenly said, standing up and moving in the direction of the enormous leather sofa.

Briscoe wanted to talk to her? This had to be a good sign. Liza wanted to skip over to the sofa, to do a little time step in joy, but that wouldn't be appropriate. This was serious theater. Walking as primly as she could, Liza sat down a few feet from Briscoe.

Briscoe studied her for a moment, steepling his fingertips in front of him.

Liza waited.

"You know," Briscoe said, extending his arm casually along the top of the couch, "you remind me of myself when I was starting out. So much raw talent just waiting to burst forth, to be shaped by a knowing hand."

Liza wanted to melt. Briscoe's reaction was better than anything she could have hoped for. Already, Liza could hear herself repeating this conversation to a very impressed Faith.

"So tell me," Briscoe said, shifting slightly so that the tips of his fingers were just grazing Liza's shoulder, "*who is* Liza Ruff? Why is she here today?"

"I want to be a star," Liza blurted truthfully, a little flustered by Briscoe's nearness. Then she wished she could bite back the words. That must have sounded so amateurish—like a naive girl from the sticks who knew nothing about the reality of theater.

"But it's more than wanting," Liza tried to explain. "It's something I just know. I was born to be on the stage. I feel at home there."

"I have no doubt," Briscoe said, his fingertips lightly stroking the leather sofa by Liza's shoulder. "You seem quite at home in the role of Lady Macbeth."

"Really?" Liza asked, feeling another rush of joy fill her chest. "Do you really think so?"

"I *believed* you," Briscoe said. "I believed you

were a mature woman with deep, conflicting emotions. That's rare in one your age. You're how old?"

"Eighteen," Liza said.

"Hmmm . . . " Briscoe said again. "Yet, you have depth. And the desire."

"Oh yes," Liza said.

Briscoe crossed his legs and leaned back against the cushions. "I'm a difficult man to work with," he said. "Very demanding."

This had to be a dream. Not only had Briscoe complimented her performance and her appearance, he was already talking as if she'd actually be working with him. Liza might not be able to repeat this conversation to Faith after all. She'd be too busy lying on the floor in a dead faint.

"I'm also very giving," Briscoe said. "But I need to know that my actors feel the same dedication I do. Otherwise, I'm wasting my time." Briscoe threw up his hands in a controlled gesture.

"Oh, I understand completely," Liza said. "If an actor doesn't give, you have nothing to work with."

"Precisely." Briscoe rose from the sofa and walked back to the desk. He leaned down and flipped through the pages of his yellow pad. "How's Sunday evening, seven P.M.?"

Liza searched his face, to make sure he was serious. Was he really asking her for a callback? "Seven's fine!" Liza said, before he could change his mind.

Briscoe straightened up and studied her intently. "You have promise," he said, "but I need to see more. I need to find out whether you truly have passion for theater."

"Oh, I do," Liza said, standing up, wishing there were some way she could prove it to him right there.

"That remains to be seen. But let's work privately together, for a bit. Then I'll be able to make my final casting decision."

"Great!" Liza said, her voice shifting upward into the brassy tones she'd been trying hard to subdue. "I'll see you then."

"A pleasure," Briscoe said, extending his hand once more and letting his eyes linger on her face.

"It's been an honor," Liza said as she felt the warm pressure of his hand. When he finally let go, she backed toward the door. "Thank you so much!"

Liza had to use every ounce of strength in her body to keep herself from running down the hall. It wasn't until she was outside and well away from the rec center that she allowed herself to give in.

"Aaaaaaaaaagh!" Liza screamed, ignoring the stares of Frisbee players and people studying on the dorm green. She took off her shoes and jumped up and down on the soft, warm grass. *"Aaaaaaaagh!"*

she screamed again. There was no other way to express how she felt right now.

Finally, someone—no, not just someone—a world-class, famous director, had said she had talent and depth!

Liza had always known there were great things ahead for her. Now she had confirmation from the best possible source. She'd only spent ten minutes with Lawrence Briscoe, but those ten minutes were going to change her life.

Eight

"Order cake . . . buy white paper tablecloth . . . napkins . . . plastic cups . . ."

Faith went over the list in her hand one last time Tuesday afternoon as she neared the supermarket. As it had for an entire week, the sun beat down on the back of her neck, on her face and hands.

"Clear glass baking dish . . . measuring spoons . . . order cake . . . "

Had she remembered everything? Faith still had five days before Melissa's engagement dinner, but she didn't want to make too many extra trips. She'd worked things out very carefully so that she'd buy the nonperishable items today, followed by beverages and condiments Thursday, and finally, Saturday, the chicken, salad ingredients, and other fresh food. That way, they could do most of the cooking the night before.

The electric glass doors slid open and Faith entered the cool relief of the supermarket. It was nice to get away from campus, to get away from that constant feeling that an axe was hanging over her head.

Erin Grant had been lurking in the halls for the past week, just waiting to pounce. Erin really seemed to dislike her. Maybe it was because Faith hadn't given her a part in her segment of the U. of S. Follies. Or maybe Erin was just lumping her together with Liza, the candle-dripping, coffee-guzzling boom box queen.

But Faith hadn't come here to think about Erin or Liza. She had work to do. The first item on her agenda was the cake. Grabbing a plastic basket from the stack by the door, Faith walked past the electronic checkout islands, toward the bakery counter. Fortunately there was no line, and a man in a white smock smiled at her from behind the counter.

"What can I do you for?" he asked.

"I'd like to order a cake for Sunday," Faith said. "Vanilla with white icing."

"How many people?"

"About a dozen. And I want it to be pretty. It's for an engagement party."

"Who's the lucky fella?"

"It's not for me," Faith said, smiling. "It's for a friend. Do you think you could put some pink and white sugar roses on top? And I'd like an inscription. 'Congratulations to Melissa and'—*Eeeek!*" Something warm and wet was rubbing against her ankle.

The man looked at Faith curiously. "What was that again?"

Faith looked down, hoping not to see a bug or something disgusting. But then she had to laugh. It was a big, friendly Labrador retriever, and he was licking her. His fur was beige, and he wore a red bandanna around his neck. Faith couldn't be sure, but he looked like the dorm dog she'd seen running around campus. But what was a dog doing in the middle of a supermarket? Wasn't that against the law?

"Uh, sorry," Faith said to the bakery man. "That was 'Melissa and Brooks.'"

"Got it," said the man. "We'll have it for you Saturday afternoon. What name should I put on the order?"

"Crowley," Faith said. Now that the order was taken care of, she could finally relax and pet the dog. "Hi there," she crooned in a loving voice. "Where did you come from, huh?"

As the dog gazed adoringly into Faith's eyes, Faith heard the rattle of metal wheels and felt strong arms grab her and lift her up.

"Hey!" Faith cried. "What—"

The next thing she knew, Faith was standing, facing Scott Sills, who grinned at her. His shaggy blond hair was pulled off his forehead by a sweatband, and his face was ruddy from the sun.

"Scott!" Faith said. He seemed so happy to see her, Faith got confused. Hadn't she yelled at him the last time she'd seen him? Hadn't she told him that things would never work out between them? So why didn't he look embarrassed or angry? "What are you doing here?"

"Max and I are spending some quality time together," Scott said, kneeling down and kissing Max's furry forehead. "I thought I'd show him around town, buy him a can of designer dog food, and maybe play some Frisbee with him later . . . but only if he lets me win. You hear that, mutt?" Scott vigorously scratched the top of Max's head, and Max wagged his tail.

Faith couldn't help smiling as she watched Scott play with the dog. No matter what his faults were, and there were plenty of them, Scott was very affectionate. And sweet. Which was what had made it so difficult, this past week, to shut him out of her mind the way she wanted to. She kept remembering how cute he'd looked in the rec center lounge, in his shorts and bare feet, and how much fun it had been to laugh at the other theater majors with him.

But she hadn't gone out of her way to see him, either. And bumping into him again, by accident, was one more reminder of why she hadn't. He wasn't the sort of person you could make plans with. He was an unpredictable flake.

"So, is Max *your* dog?" Faith asked. "I thought he didn't belong to anybody."

"He doesn't," Scott said, "though a bunch of us make sure he gets enough to eat."

"That's nice of you."

"Max is a good guy," Scott said, looking over at the dog, who was sniffing around an open box of graham crackers that had spilled onto the floor. With a glance to his right and his left, Max started licking up the crumbs as quickly as he could.

"Yo, Max!" Scott said, rushing forward to pull the dog away. "You want us to get kicked out of here?"

"I'm sure they're going to kick you out anyway," Faith said. "Dogs aren't allowed in supermarkets."

"But Max is so harmless," Scott said. "I'm sure they'll make an exception for him." He smiled winningly at Faith. "So, I guess you followed us here to tell us you changed your mind."

"Changed my mind about what?"

"About our relationship," Scott said, his amber eyes wide and round. "Well, I'm happy to inform you that you haven't wasted your time. I'm still available. So is Max."

Faith started to laugh, but she stopped herself. She knew exactly what Scott was trying to do. He was trying to charm her into forgetting the fact that she lived by a set of unbending rules. He was trying to make her forget how angry she still was with him. But Faith would never forget. *You're not Mr. Right. You're not Mr. Right,* Faith silently told him, clenching her fists.

"Sorry," she told Scott. "Meeting you here was a total accident. I'm buying stuff for my friend's engagement party."

"Oh yeah. That big dinner you're planning." Scott's eyes grew thoughtful for a moment, then they brightened. "Well, it must have been fate that we bumped into each other."

Typical Scott answer. And one more reminder of why things could never work out between them. They were too different. Scott *believed* in accidents, in bending the rules, and in flying by the seat of his pants. Faith had learned she couldn't live like that. That was how she'd ended up on probation.

"It's *not* the same," Faith said. "Planning something's not the same as leaving it up to chance. And I've got to plan my life from now on, so I don't get in trouble again."

"I don't blame you for wanting to be careful," Scott said, starting to push his cart down the aisle. "I know you're still spooked by that probation thing. But you can't plan *everything* in life."

"Well, maybe not *everything*," Faith conceded as she walked beside the cart, past the brightly colored boxes and cellophane-wrapped packages, "but—"

"Think how boring it would be if you knew every single thing that was ever going to happen to you. When you were going to get married, and who, what you were going to turn out to be, when you were going to die . . . "

It *was* a scary thought. It reminded Faith of how she'd felt before she'd met Scott: As if her whole life was predictable and dull. As if nothing exciting was ever going to happen to her.

Scott turned left at the dairy case. The air was colder here, and Faith felt goosebumps rise on her bare arms. Max scampered ahead toward the meat section, licking his chops.

"My parents are planners," Scott said as they walked. "My brother and sister, too. They've all got those little leather datebooks with everything scheduled for months in advance. When they're going to eat, sleep, brush their teeth. But ask me if they ever enjoy themselves, if they ever do anything just for fun."

"Do they?" Faith asked, though she knew what the answer was going to be. Listening to Scott was making her even more confused. She could tell from the way Scott described his family that they weren't happy, yet they were living exactly the way Faith was trying to. Faith didn't have a datebook, but she had lists posted all over her room. Lists for Melissa's engagement dinner, lists of goals, both short-term and long-term, lists of dorm regulations and countless others. But looking at it through Scott's eyes, she suddenly felt foolish.

"Let's go for a ride," Scott said, his amber eyes twinkling.

"Where?" Faith asked. Maybe she could spend a *little* time with him. After all, this wasn't a date, and it wasn't as if she'd gone out of her way to find him. This was just an accidental meeting.

"Right here," Scott said. "We'll help you do your grocery shopping."

"Uh-oh," Faith said. "You couldn't possibly mean—"

Scott grabbed her by the waist and dumped her right into the empty cart.

"Scott!" Faith wailed, her body folding up like an

accordion. "I'm too old to ride in a shopping cart!"

"You're never too old," Scott said, pushing the metal cart at high speed down the empty aisle. Max, who'd been nosing through the steaks, came running back, his toenails clicking against the linoleum floor.

"Scott!" Faith wailed, clutching the metal mesh sides. "Slow down!"

"Sure." Scott dug the heels of his sneakers into the floor, and the cart stopped short. Faith lurched forward, then gave Scott a dirty look.

"Why do I have the feeling I'm in big trouble?" Faith asked.

"Give me your list," Scott said, taking it from her hand. "Let's see how fast we can find everything so we can get outside. This fluorescent light will kill your eyes. Let's see. What's the first thing? White paper tablecloth. Ready?"

Before Faith could answer, Scott gave the cart a mighty shove, and Faith went flying down the aisle, heading straight for a pyramid of canned green beans.

"Scott!" Faith screamed, but he dashed after the cart, turning it at the last second to avoid a collision. Max barked in glee as he ran after them.

"Quiet, Max!" Scott warned his pal, as he pushed the cart in a swerving line down the back aisle by the freezer section. "You don't want the manager to hear you. He'll throw you out on your tail."

"Come on, Scott," Faith begged, as a cold breeze whipped through her hair. "I'm getting car sick!"

"Paper goods!" Scott crowed triumphantly, popping a wheelie at the end of aisle five. "Just what we're looking for."

The cart crashed down again with a thump, and Faith laced her fingers through the holes so she wouldn't lurch around so much. It was actually sort of fun getting to ride through a grocery store again. She hadn't done it since she was a kid, and she hadn't realized how much she missed it.

"Quick!" Scott shouted as they neared the paper tablecloths and napkins. "Try to grab what you want as I pass by so we don't have to slow down."

Faith tried to kneel in the cart so she could reach for the plastic-covered packages as they zoomed by. She managed to grab a tablecloth and napkins, but the tablecloth was the wrong size and the napkins didn't match it.

"Wait!" Faith cried as they careened down the aisle. "I didn't get the right thing."

"We'll come back," Scott shouted. "What's next?"

"A glass baking dish for—"

Faith gasped in mid-sentence. A tall, heavyset man in a turquoise smock turned the corner and was heading straight toward them.

"It's the manager!" Scott said in a hoarse whisper. "Hide!"

"How?" Faith started to ask, but Scott covered her with rolls of paper towels. "What about Max?" she asked. But it was too late. The manager had already seen the dog.

"No animals in the store," the manager said. "You'll have to leave."

"Try not to think of him as a dog," Scott said. "He has very human emotions."

"Out!" the manager said, pointing toward the door. "Your girlfriend, too."

Faith poked her head up above the paper towels. "Sorry."

The manager wasn't even listening. He turned around and headed back to the front of the store. Faith breathed a sigh of relief. At least she hadn't gotten in trouble on campus. And the manager hadn't seemed that angry. Faith was almost certain she'd seen a glimmer of a smile on his face.

"At least give me a ride to the door," Faith said as Scott put back all the paper towels.

"But at a much more dignified speed," Scott said as he strutted down the aisle, pushing the cart. "We *are* adults, after all."

"Very young, very immature adults," Faith said with a giggle as they passed some shelves filled with wine bottles.

"Hey!" Scott said. "You need some wine for your party? We could use our fake IDs to buy it."

The giggle got caught in Faith's throat and she glared at Scott. How could he be so insensitive after all she'd been through? How could he make a joke about liquor? Faith was almost more disappointed than angry. Every time she started to warm up to Scott, he did something to remind her how wrong he was for her.

"I'm sorry," Scott said. "That wasn't funny."

"No, it wasn't," Faith said. "I'll have enough to worry about at the dinner without worrying about alcohol. I'm on probation. I can't even go near a bottle of rubbing alcohol while I'm on campus. And we can't serve alcohol at the dinner anyway, because of Melissa's father. He's and al—"

Faith stopped herself. She had promised not to reveal Melissa's secret to anyone.

"Say no more," Scott said, wheeling quickly past the wine display. "I understand. As of now, we won't even think or talk about alcohol."

Scott lifted her gently out of the cart, and Max nuzzled her with his cold, wet nose.

"Why don't we wait outside while you finish your shopping," Scott said. "Then we'll walk you back to campus."

As Scott and Max headed out the door, Faith took the cart and started looking for the things on her list. She'd been impressed by how quickly Scott had backed off from the whole subject of alcohol. Maybe he was flaky, but he wasn't completely insensitive. Faith smiled as she filled the shopping cart, thinking about her speedier trip down these same aisles. For the first time since being put on probation, Faith had actually had fun.

As the cashier rang up her purchases, Faith noticed Scott and Max pressing their faces against the glass front of the store. She smiled at them and felt her heart melt, just a little.

"Can you hold on a second?" Faith asked the cashier. "I'll be right back." Faith ran to the dog food section, grabbed a few cans of Le Pup, and added them to her purchases.

"Let me carry those for you," Scott offered as Faith emerged from the store with her grocery bags.

Faith handed Scott one of her bags, and she carried the other.

"It was nice of you to get the dog food," Scott said, looking into the bag he was carrying. "But you really didn't have to spend so much. I was only kidding about getting designer dog food."

"I wanted to thank you for helping me shop."

"Well, I know you've got that big dinner to plan.

You can't do it all yourself."

Faith hesitated. Scott seemed to be hinting that he still wanted to help her with Melissa's party. Should she take him up on it? There was an awful lot of work to do.

"What kind of restaurants did you work in?" Faith asked, trying to sound neutral.

"I worked in a really nice one, one summer in high school," Scott said. "Of course, I was just a busboy, but I learned a lot watching the professional waiters. There's a special way to do everything, like fold a napkin, pour a drink . . . "

"Think you still remember?" Faith asked.

"Sure!" Scott said, his face breaking into a happy grin. He shifted his groceries to his left arm, and put his right arm around Faith. Though it was just as hot outside as it had been before, Faith didn't mind the feel of his warm skin against hers. It felt natural to have his arm there. Natural, and a little exciting.

But of course she wasn't going to do or say anything to encourage him. If he wanted to leave his arm there, fine, but that was as far as he was going to get. Faith forced herself not to look at Scott until they'd reached campus and climbed the stairs to the second floor of Coleridge Hall.

"So," Scott said when they arrived at her door. Max settled down on the floor nearby, closed his eyes, and almost immediately began snoring.

"So," Faith said, lowering her grocery bag.

Scott put his bag down, too. "What do we do now?" He was staring at Faith with a simple direct-ness that made her heart pound. But she couldn't let him see what an effect he was having on her. She had to resist. Otherwise he'd think . . .

Faith didn't care what he thought. She moved close to Scott so that their faces were just a few inches apart. Scott's eyes glowed, and his lips parted slightly. Faith tilted her head back, but then some-thing caught her eye. It was a piece of paper tacked to her door. The paper had an official look to it. An official, *familiar* look.

Faith froze as she read the tiny print.

University of Springfield
Citation

Faith Crowley and Liza Ruff of Coleridge Hall, Room *219* are hereby charged with *leaving three burning candles unattended in room, dripping onto school property and posing serious fire hazard to all residents of the building. While this is a minor infraction of dormitory regulations, Faith Crowley's probation status requires her appearance before the peer review board, Monday*, 3:00P.M.

Signed,
Erin Grant, Resident Adviser

"Oh no," Faith groaned, pulling the citation off the door.

"What's the matter?" Scott asked, startled.

Max, sensing the tension, immediately awoke from his nap and looked up at them questioningly.

Faith handed Scott the citation so he could read it. "Liza left her candles burning again. She could have started a fire! And *I'm* the one who's going to get punished."

"But you didn't do anything," Scott protested.

"It doesn't matter," Faith said. "At least not to Erin. It's a *room* violation, and I live in the room, so I share responsibility."

"That's not fair!" Scott sympathized. He put his arms comfortingly around Faith, but she couldn't even feel them. Her whole body was starting to go numb as the truth began to sink in. The end had come. The second she'd let her guard down, she'd been caught. It was almost as if Erin had seen her fooling around in the supermarket, and this was her punishment.

Faith felt a sharp, stabbing pain in her stomach. "You know what they're going to do to me? They're going to bring my parents in for a conference, which means my parents are going to find out about the fake ID, which means my parents will never trust me again as long as they live, not to mention the fact that I'll probably have to give up all my extracurricular activities, so I can just kiss my drama career goodbye. You can't be a drama major if you don't work on any shows. I'm supposed to meet Lawrence Briscoe Friday to see about working on his crew for *Macbeth,* but now I shouldn't even bother."

"It can't be that bad," Scott insisted, squeezing her tighter.

Faith struggled to break free of his grip. "How would you know?" she asked. "You're so slippery, you never get caught."

"Hey," Scott said, "this isn't my fault."

"Of course it's your fault," Faith ranted. "If I hadn't gotten that other citation, I wouldn't have to worry about this now. I should have known better than to give you another chance. Being with you only leads to one thing—trouble. Just please get out of here before you make it even worse."

Scott stared at her, his eyes filled with hurt.

"Oh, and in case you thought you were helping out at Melissa's dinner? Forget it. I wouldn't let you near that place if you begged me. You'd probably spike Mr. McDormand's drink."

"Faith!"

"I don't have anything else to say to you," Faith

said, digging around in the grocery bags for the cans of dog food. She was furious at herself for her own stupidity. She'd already realized Scott wasn't her Mr. Right. Why had she even wasted her time with him this afternoon?

"Here!" Faith said, shoving the cans into Scott's hands. "Now take your dog and go away!"

Nine

....

"Can't you at least give me a hint?" Brooks asked Melissa, Thursday afternoon, as the two of them cut across the parking lot next to the gym.

Brooks wore khaki shorts and a button-down short sleeve oxford shirt. His arms and legs were thick and muscular from soccer and mountain climbing, and his blond curly hair was even lighter than usual from all the time he'd spent in the sun lately.

All Melissa wanted to do, though, was get out of the hot sun. She'd just taken a shower after her two-hour workout with Brooks, and she was already sticky and uncomfortable. Or maybe it wasn't the sun that was making her uncomfortable. Maybe it was the fact that for the past two hours, Brooks kept bringing up the subject of their engagement party even though Melissa had already made it very clear she didn't want to discuss it with him.

"I've already told you," Melissa said irritably as the pavement gave way to grass. "You'll find out everything you need to know when we get to the student union."

Faith, wonderful Faith, had figured out all the arrangements for the dinner on Sunday, and she'd called a meeting at the student union today for the people involved. Though Melissa was grateful to everyone for volunteering to help, she was very nervous about facing them all at once. Even if Faith hadn't told them the *real* reason they were holding the dinner on campus, they still could have pieced the story together.

When Melissa walked into the room, would they all be staring at her in pity? Would they be thinking *Poor Melissa! Her parents have no money and her father's a drunk. Let's be kind to her by throwing this party.*

Melissa was starting to feel nauseous. Maybe she'd made a big mistake letting Faith do this. All she'd done was trade the charity of Brooks's parents for the charity of her friends.

Brooks took Melissa's hand as they crossed the grassy expanse of lawn, heading towards McLaren

Plaza. The grass was starting to turn brown from day after day of relentless sunshine, and the trees they passed looked dry and brittle.

"Look, Melissa," Brooks said, squeezing her fingers, "I know you want to feel totally independent and plan this dinner without me. And I haven't tried to get involved, have I? Haven't I let you run things?"

"Yes," Melissa admitted. "But you've certainly asked enough questions about it."

"Well, it's my party, too, isn't it?" Brooks asked. "I'm allowed to know what's going on."

Melissa felt a pang of guilt mixed in with the nausea. Of course Brooks was right. He had every right to know. But Melissa was afraid that once he found out, he'd still try to take charge, to make her feel like poor, helpless Melissa who'd been rescued from poverty by Prince Charming.

"The food's all taken care of, and the decorations, and the place," Melissa said. "There's nothing you need to worry about."

By now, they'd reached the cobbled brick of McLaren Plaza. It was a little cooler here because it was shaded by cherry trees, but the air was heavy and thick with their sweet, cloying perfume.

"I don't care so much about the food and details like that," Brooks said as they approached the cast-iron statue of Derek C. Brock, the founding president of the university. "But I think we should talk about our families. You know, try to anticipate any problems that might come up."

"What's that supposed to mean?" Melissa asked, feeling anger coil around the guilt and nausea.

"I just mean, maybe you could give me a few pointers I could pass along to my parents. For instance, what are your parents' interests? What would be some good topics of conversation?"

Melissa glared at Brooks. That wasn't what he really meant. He really wanted to know whether he should tell his parents that her father was a drunk. Whether they should dress down so her parents wouldn't feel too conspicuously shabby.

"What's the matter?" Brooks asked. "Why are you looking at me like that?"

All the swirling anger, guilt, and nausea was beginning to make Melissa feel dizzy. She paused at the base of the statue and leaned against it for support. Getting married was supposed to be such a happy time. So why did she feel as if she was going to pass out?

"Here's what you can tell your parents," Melissa said, struggling to sound calm and normal. "Just tell them to show up at the student union at six o'clock on Sunday."

"But what about your parents?" Brooks asked. "What should I say about them?"

"Why are you so obsessed with my parents?" Melissa shouted. "Why do your parents have to know *anything* about them?"

"I'm *not* obsessed with them," Brooks protested. "I just thought—"

"Please don't think anymore!" Melissa begged. "Just let me handle things, okay?"

"Okay, okay!" Brooks said. He started to move forward to give Melissa a hug, but he stopped himself. "Look," he said, running a hand distractedly through his blond curls. "Maybe it would be better if I didn't come to this meeting."

Melissa felt instantly remorseful. She hadn't meant to drive Brooks away.

"It's okay," she said. "You can come. It's just that—"

"No," Brooks said. "I'll just let you handle it, as you said. Why don't I meet you in front of the student union in half an hour. Will that be enough time?"

Melissa nodded contritely. "I'm sorry I yelled."

Brooks shrugged. "They say getting married can be a stressful time. It's right up there with losing a job and illness in the family. We'll just chalk it up to stress, okay?"

Melissa gave Brooks a quick kiss on the lips. "I'll meet you at five-thirty." Turning, she ran from Brooks across the uneven cobbled bricks toward the student union. Faith had said they'd be meeting in the main room. Taking the three front steps in one bound, Melissa pushed open the double doors and raced down the hall.

The main room was large and brightly lit, with concrete pillars dividing the space at regular intervals. Round white Formica tables filled the space, surrounded by hard black metal chairs.

"Melissa!" Faith's voice called out. "Over here!"

Melissa noticed Faith sitting at a table at the far end of the room, near the aluminum and glass snack bar. Sitting with her were Winnie, Lauren, KC, and Peter. As Melissa approached them, she studied all the faces. Did they look as if they felt sorry for her? It was hard to tell.

"Sit down, bride-to-be," Faith said, pulling up a chair. "Where's the husband-to-be?"

Melissa hesitated. She couldn't tell them the truth. They'd just wonder why the newlyweds were already fighting. "He couldn't make it," she said. "He's got a paper due tomorrow, and he still has a lot of work left to do."

"Looks like Brooks is losing the old touch," Winnie joked. "Back in high school, he'd have had that paper finished days ago."

Melissa felt her stomach lurch. Had Winnie seen through her story? Melissa tried to get her off the subject of Brooks. "Nice outfit," she said to Winnie, who was wearing a T-shirt that said "Jamaican Bobsled Team" with a picture of a toboggan and lots of snow. "Let me guess. Is it your 'Think Cool' outfit?"

"Exactly," Winnie said, taking a sip of soda from a frosty can. "The only way you can escape the heat is by using your imagination."

"Too bad you can't escape the rest of reality that way," Faith said. "Maybe I could think myself onto a campus where I didn't feel like an outlaw."

Melissa had to smile, even though she knew how much Faith was suffering over her latest citation. The last thing Faith looked like was an outlaw. She wore a pink eyelet sundress, and her blond hair was pulled up into a high ponytale tied with a pink satin ribbon.

"When do you have to go before the board?" asked Peter. His chair was pulled up so close to KC's that they were practically sitting on each other's laps.

"Monday afternoon," Faith said glumly. "I just know they're going to kick me out of school."

"I'm sure it won't be *that* bad," said Lauren, who sat on Faith's other side. Her wispy hair was pulled off her forehead with a wide black headband, and she wore an antiquey-looking patchwork vest buttoned all the way up so that it served as a shirt. "This was just a room violation, and it wasn't even your fault."

"Tell it to the peer review board," Faith said. "At

the very least, they're going to call my parents in. But let's try to think about something pleasant."

"Yes," KC said. "Like Peter's award. I guess everyone's heard the good news by now?" KC turned her beautiful face toward Peter and gazed at him. Her gray eyes were so warm, so proud and loving. Peter returned her gaze, though his eyes seemed a little sad.

"Congratulations, Peter," Melissa said. "Sounds like your career is off and running."

"Thanks."

"Say, Peter, I'd like to do a piece on you and the Morgan Grant," Lauren said, pushing up her wire-rimmed glasses. "Do you think we could talk sometime this week?"

"Sure," Peter said, "but I'm surprised you have time. Aren't you writing your His and Hers column with Dash?"

Winnie screwed up her face and covered her ears with her hands. "Don't say that horrible name around here," she said. "His name is dirt as far as everybody's concerned, right?"

"Right!" chimed in Faith and KC.

"I'll find the time," Lauren assured Peter. "My first article's almost finished. It's amazing how much more free time I have to write now that I'm. . ." Lauren's voice faltered. "Well, it's almost finished."

"Why don't we get down to business," Faith said, making her voice sound extra cheerful. She leaned down and pulled a notebook out of her book bag. She opened it, and Melissa saw several pages of lists written in Faith's neat handwriting. "Now, most of you already know your assignments, but I'd like to go over them just to make sure we haven't left anything or anyone out."

"I know what I'm doing," KC said. "I'm going to borrow dishes and utensils from the Tri Betas."

Faith made a check mark on her list. "It's really nice of your sorority to lend all that expensive stuff. It sure beats paper plates and plastic utensils."

"Hey," KC said, "this is a dinner party, not a picnic. We just have to be really careful not to break anything or we'll have to replace it."

"Gotcha," Faith said. "Now, Kimberly and her boyfriend, Derek, are going to cook the main course using a recipe from the Angelettis' restaurant which, in case you didn't know, has the best health food west of the Rockies."

KC made a face. "Don't worry," she assured Melissa. "It's not vegetarian. In fact, this recipe is something even *I* like, and I hate health food."

"Barney Sharfenburger will be in charge of the chairs," Faith continued going down her list. "Peter will be the official staff photographer, and Lauren will run cleanup. Winnie and Josh will set up, provide flowers, and make computer-inspired decorations."

"What kind of decorations?" Lauren asked Winnie.

"You'll see," Winnie said mysteriously.

"Uh-oh," KC said. "Why do I have the feeling we're going to see repeating patterns of giant happy faces?"

Melissa felt as if she was watching a five-way Ping-Pong match as she listened to all these plans. There were so many people and so many jobs to be done that she couldn't keep track. She barely knew half the people they'd mentioned. She knew Kimberly lived next door to Faith, and Derek was Kimberly's boyfriend, but she barely knew Peter or Lauren.

Why should all these people be so willing to help her? She hadn't done anything to deserve it. Look how she'd just spoken to Brooks, her fiancé. She'd been more than rude. She'd been awful. She'd made him suffer just because she felt so insecure.

That wasn't fair. Brooks had only treated her with kindness. So why couldn't she trust him? Why couldn't she admit what she was really afraid of, so he could comfort her and tell her her fears were foolish? Then they'd both feel better.

Melissa was just grateful that Brooks had been so understanding and patient up until now. And she was even *more* grateful that this terrifying family dinner would be over soon.

"So I guess that wraps it up," Faith said, a few minutes later, closing her notebook and putting it back in her book bag.

Winnie barely heard. She was too fascinated by what was going on across the table. KC and Peter looked as if they'd literally grown together, their arms and legs twining around each other like vines. It was hard to tell where one began and the other left off.

"You clear on your assignment?" Faith asked Winnie. "I didn't see you write it down."

"I got it, I got it," Winnie answered, growing irritated with Faith's obsession with lists and planning. Besides, Winnie was more interested in watching KC and Peter than she was in writing stuff down.

The looks that passed between them were amazing. It was almost as if they were speaking without words, and each understood the other perfectly. Even Winnie could almost understand them, the feelings were so intense. KC was saying Peter would never really be far away from her in her heart. Peter was saying that he might not have the strength to leave her after all.

Just watching them, Winnie felt close to tears. They were going to miss each other so much. Or maybe her tears were for herself. How long had it been since Winnie had felt anything that intensely with Josh? Winnie couldn't remember. And Josh never looked at her anymore the way Peter looked at KC.

"Bye, Winnie," called several voices. Winnie waved at whoever it was.

When had she and Josh lost the fire? Not too many months ago, after they'd broken up the first time, Winnie had nearly lost her mind. She could barely function without him. Then, when they'd gotten back together, Winnie had felt like the happiest person on the planet.

Winnie was still happy with Josh, but she didn't feel those highs and lows anymore—just a flat, mellow line. It was a good thing she wasn't a heart patient, Winnie thought to herself, or that flat line would mean she was dead. But this was almost as bad.

"You coming, Win?" Melissa asked.

Winnie looked up and suddenly realized that everyone else had gone. "Uh, yeah. . ." she said, hopping up. "You going back to Forest Hall?"

"Actually, no. Brooks is meeting me outside and we're going to go to the library and study."

"I thought he was writing a paper," Winnie said. "Didn't you say—"

"I gotta go," Melissa said. "I'll see you later."

Melissa's reaction seemed a little strange, but Winnie didn't wonder too long about it. Her mind was already back on her uneventful relationship with Josh. All the time she'd been suffering through their breakups, she'd longed for a time when they could just enjoy each other's company without any problems. Now that she had that, she was totally bored. They couldn't stay like this forever, could they?

Maybe they were just going through a phase, Winnie thought as she left the student union and jogged across the green back to her dorm. Maybe passion ebbed and flowed like the tide. The tide had already gone out. So any minute, now, the tide would come back in, sweeping her away in a wave of turbulent, exciting emotions.

Winnie felt better already. Josh was probably in his room right now, eagerly waiting for her to return from the meeting. When he saw her, he'd drop whatever he was doing, grab her, and kiss her the way he had when they'd first met.

Winnie hurried down the hill toward Forest Hall, part of a complex of sterile-looking cement buildings nicknamed "The Motels," which sat at the bottom of a gentle slope. She threw herself through the front doors, nearly strangling herself on the volleyball net that had been set up in the middle of the lobby. No one was using the net at the moment, so there was no one Winnie could yell at. It didn't matter, anyway. Josh was waiting for her. Winnie dashed up the stairs to the second floor and knocked on his door.

"It's open!" Josh called.

clickclickclick. clickclickclickclickclick. clickclickclick.

Winnie threw the door open and saw Josh sitting in front of his computer, typing rapidly as he stared like a zombie into his monitor. The electric fan on the shelf above his computer blew his longish brown hair straight back, and his long legs were propped up on a carton of printer paper beneath his desk.

"I'm back!" Winnie announced, waiting expectantly in the doorway.

"Hey, Win," Josh said, his eyes still glued to his monitor. His fingers flew over the keyboard as he typed words that were unintelligible to Winnie.

"Well?" Winnie asked, disappointed. It was bad enough he hadn't asked her about the meeting, but he'd barely even noticed she was there.

"Hmmm?" Josh asked as his fingers tapped quickly and lightly.

clickclickclickclick. clickclickclick. clickclickclickclick

"How was the meeting, you ask?" Winnie said, dragging over the desk chair of Josh's roommate, Mikoto, and sitting beside Josh. "Well, Josh, it was very informative. And what will *we* be doing for the party, Winnie? Well, Josh, we'll be setting the table, buying flowers, and designing decorations on your computer."

The clicking paused for a few seconds, and Josh grinned in amusement. "Sorry," he said. "I guess I'm not much of a conversationalist at the moment. I'm just really involved in this project."

"No problem," Winnie said. "I enjoyed playing both parts."

Josh gave Winnie a peck on the cheek. "You're cute," he said.

About as cute as an old shoe, Winnie thought as Josh immediately resumed his typing. What was wrong with them? Why *couldn't* they have what KC and Peter had? Of course, it was possible that KC and Peter's feelings were sharpened by the fact that they'd soon be thousands of miles apart. Nothing like time and distance to make you appreciate someone.

Hey! Maybe that was it! Maybe Winnie should go to Europe. She'd spent last summer in Paris, and she'd always wanted to go back. And if Josh knew she was leaving, maybe he'd react the way KC had. He'd realize the value of what he was about to lose, if only temporarily. That should put the romance back into their romance. It had worked for KC and Peter. Now Winnie would make it work for Josh and her.

Ten
....

The rec center lounge was so hot and stuffy on Friday, Faith thought she was going to suffocate. Of course, with this never-ending heat wave, every place on campus was hot, inside and out, but this room was even worse. There were no windows, no air-conditioning, not even a fan.

So much for looking fresh and pretty to meet Lawrence Briscoe. Faith had borrowed a sleeveless white linen dress from KC, and Lauren's pearls, so that she'd look creative yet sophisticated. Now her dress was sticking to her back and her legs were sticking to the vinyl sofa.

Not that it mattered what she looked like. She wasn't here to audition for a part. She was interested in the assistant director position. The chance to work with a great director like Briscoe would be an incredible learning experience. Even if she just got to be a stagehand, she'd still be able to watch him work.

"You're up, Faith," said Meredith Paxton, popping his head in the door of the lounge.

Faith smiled up at her friend. She and Meredith had worked crew together on several shows.

"You nervous about meeting the great one?" Meredith asked Faith as he walked her down the hall.

Faith almost laughed. Ordinarily, her answer would have been a big fat yes, but she'd been so distracted lately that she'd barely given a thought to this interview with Lawrence Briscoe. All she could think about was her upcoming appearance before the review board. Faith had been having nightmares about it every night since she'd gotten the citation from Erin.

It had been the same nightmare every night. Faith was wheeled in a grocery cart into a dark room lit only by drippy candles. High above her, glaring down, was a tribunal of judges in long black robes and powdered wigs. Only these weren't the regular peer review judges. This tribunal was made up of Erin, Scott, and Liza. And when it was time to announce the punishment, they all started yelling at once. Erin was screaming that Faith would never work on another show again, and Scott was shouting that Faith wasn't any fun, and Liza was still reciting her letter speech from *Macbeth,* while spraying herself with cheap perfume.

"Faith Crowley," Meredith announced as he poked his head into a doorway.

Faith was tempted to tell Meredith to scratch her name off the list, but that wouldn't be very professional. As long as she was here, she might as well go through with it. Putting on what she hoped looked like a genuine smile, Faith entered the tastefully furnished office. It looked more like a den, with its richly colored Persian rug and a leather sofa so big you could get swallowed up in it.

"Lawrence Briscoe," said the young Englishman rising behind the mahogany desk. Physically, he was the opposite of Scott—slim and dark and meticulously dressed. He looked impossibly fresh and crisp, despite the heat, in a white, open-necked polo shirt. His high cheekbones and deepset eyes gave him a dramatic, brooding appearance.

"How do you do," Faith said. "I'm a great admirer of your work."

"And I'm a great admirer of your beauty," Briscoe said, extending his hand for Faith to shake and clasping it warmly. "That's a lovely dress you're wearing."

Faith smiled as Briscoe gestured for her to sit on a chair in front of the desk while he leaned back against it.

"So tell me," he said, his eyes flitting over her, "what do you feel you could contribute to this production?"

"Well, I've already directed several shows this year and I'd like to continue working in that area—but mostly I'd like to learn from you."

Briscoe moved away from the desk and sat in the chair beside Faith. "And what do you think I could teach you?"

"Oh, everything," Faith said. "I'd like to see how you work with the actors, how you get performances out of them, and how you communicate your vision to them. And I'd like to know how you work out your staging."

"I could teach you many things," Briscoe said, staring directly into her eyes.

His stare was making Faith a little uncomfortable. If Faith didn't know better, she'd have thought he was flirting with her, but that was impossible. She was just a college freshman.

"So tell me something of yourself," Briscoe said, leaning back in his chair and pressing his fingertips together. "*Who is* Faith Crowley? Which plays has she directed?"

"Well, I assistant-directed a musical, *Stop the World, I Want to Get Off,* and actually had quite a lot of creative input with staging and production design. Then I directed my own experimental version of *Alice in Wonderland* using children from a local day-care center. I also directed a musical segment of the U. of S. Follies, which was basically a musical revue."

"Quite a range of experience," Briscoe said, making a notation on a yellow legal pad, "though you've had no Shakespeare."

Maybe he wasn't flirting. Maybe Faith was uncomfortable because there was such a drastic difference between them. He was an accomplished director with a dozen plays to his credit, and she was just a freshman drama major who might not even finish the school year, let alone follow in his footsteps.

"Oh, I know that's very different," Faith said, "but I'd be willing to work very hard."

"I would expect no less," Briscoe said. "If you were my assistant, you'd be at my beck and call night and day. I'm very demanding."

Briscoe gave her that look again and Faith began to wonder exactly what he meant by "night."

"You know," Briscoe said, looking at her fondly,

"you remind me of myself when I was starting out. So much raw talent just waiting to burst forth, to be shaped by a knowing hand."

Faith was getting that uncomfortable feeling again. Looking at his long, slender fingers, she got the feeling that his "knowing hands" had shaped a lot of raw talents like herself. And the last thing she needed was to get involved with a visiting professor. Talk about breaking the rules!

"I have to be completely honest with you," Faith said, avoiding eye contact. "My time may be somewhat limited because I'm on probation right now."

"I beg your pardon?" Briscoe asked, raising his eyebrows.

"Probation," Faith said. "I sort of got in trouble recently, so my extracurricular activities may be somewhat limited."

"What kind of trouble?" Briscoe asked, leaning forward in his chair so that his knees were almost touching hers. His eyes glittered with interest.

There was no point in hiding the truth even if it meant not getting to work on the show. "I used a fake ID to buy alcohol," she said. "I got caught by a campus security guard."

Briscoe rested a hand lightly on her bare leg. "How very interesting." Then a crease appeared in his brow and he quickly withdrew his hand. "So I take it you're not old enough to buy alcohol legally?"

"Not in this state," Faith said. "The drinking age is twenty-one."

"And you are. . ."

"Eighteen," Faith said. "That's old enough to vote and serve in the army. I don't see why they have different rules for alcohol."

"Oh, yes," Briscoe said. "It's quite obvious you have the depth and substance of a mature woman. That's rare in someone your age. But you like to have a good time, eh?" He winked and smiled, revealing two even rows of tiny white teeth.

"Well, I broke the rules, if that's what you mean," Faith said, crossing her arms in front of her chest. "And if I ever get caught with alcohol again, I'll get expelled from school."

Briscoe positively beamed at her. "Let's chat," he said, standing up and walking toward the leather sofa. He sat down and patted the cushions next to him.

"I thought we *were* chatting," Faith said, staying glued to her chair. She didn't like his reaction to her probation problem at all. He was acting as if she were a "bad girl," so what was to stop her from a little more bad behavior? He had some nerve stereotyping her that way. And famous director or not, he had some nerve expecting her to give in to him just five minutes after they'd met.

"Do I *intimidate* you?" Briscoe asked. "I haven't meant to. Try not to think of me as a director. Try to think of me as a friend. We're not so far apart in age, after all."

"I'm quite comfortable where I am," Faith said, gritting her teeth.

"Dear Faith, I *have* intimidated you," Briscoe said, rising and going to his chair behind the desk. "I'm so very sorry. I'm afraid I'm quite out of my element here, in the U. S. of A. I'm not sure how to talk to people."

Faith was confused. Was he backpedaling since she hadn't responded to his overtures? Or had she just misunderstood? Faith's experience with guys was very limited, and she certainly didn't have any experience with *men*. Especially not sophisticated men like Briscoe.

"I really must move on to my next interview," Briscoe said, his tone businesslike. He flipped through his yellow notebook and picked up his pencil. "But I would like to schedule a callback appointment so we can discuss things further. Why don't you come back tomorrow evening, so we can speak privately. I need to know that my crew feels the same dedication I do, the same passion for theater."

Now Faith didn't know what to think. *Passion for theater*? If that wasn't a pickup line, what was? It was right up there with all those other clichés like "Want to see my etchings?" Who did this man think he was, taking advantage of his position to seduce young girls? He was just one more creep to add to her growing list, just one more Mr. Wrong.

"I certainly do have a passion for theater," Faith said, jumping to her feet, "but not the kind you mean."

"I'm sure I don't know what you're talking about," Briscoe said.

"Don't play dumb with me," Faith said. "You've been dropping hints ever since I walked in here. What kind of a sucker do you take me for? I'm not meeting you tomorrow night or any other night! I know what you're *really* after. Well, let me tell you right now—you're not getting it from me!"

As Briscoe stared after her, Faith stormed out of the office and slammed the door behind her.

Eleven

"What's wrong with you?" Liza yelled at herself as she paced the short distance between her bed and Faith's.

Liza had been rehearsing her *Macbeth* monologue, trying to recreate the emotional intensity she'd had at her reading for Lawrence Briscoe, but it was impossible to find again. Maybe it was the lighting that was destroying the atmosphere. How was she supposed to feel like a queen of the Middle Ages with fluorescent lights buzzing overhead? Liza *needed* her candles to get in the mood, but she didn't dare. Faith would throw a fit.

"You're losing it, Liza," she tried to bully herself. "You're never going to be a star this way."

Catching a glimpse of her reflection in the full-length mirror, Liza shook her head. Because of the dreadful heat, and Faith's strong warnings *not* to use the electric fan, Liza couldn't wear her velvet robe anymore. Instead, she was stuck wearing her shorty pink terrycloth bathrobe, not exactly an outfit for Lady Macbeth.

Someone tapped softly on the door. "Faith? You in there?" It sounded like Kimberly, their next-door neighbor.

"She's not here," Liza called irritably. Why were the visitors always for Faith? Why didn't anyone ever stop by to see her?

"Can I leave her a message?" Kimberly asked.

With a sigh of disgust, Liza opened the door. "I'm trying to rehearse," she said.

Kimberly's pretty face was contrite. Her black hair was pulled up tight into a bun, and she wore a white leotard with white cotton shorts over it. Tall and very slender, she still looked like a dance major, though she'd recently decided to change her major to physics.

"I'm sorry to interrupt," Kimberly said. "Could you just tell Faith one thing for me?"

"What?" Liza blocked the doorway with her body to discourage Kimberly from staying a second longer than necessary.

Kimberly backed up a step. "Tell her not to worry about finding us a hot plate. Derek has a friend off-campus with a fully equipped kitchen, so we'll be able to do all our cooking there. We'll prepare all the hot stuff tomorrow night, then all we'll have to do is reheat it in the microwave at the rec center."

"I hope I can remember all that," Liza said grumpily.

"I could write it down," Kimberly offered.

"No," Liza said, already closing the door. She was eager to get back to work. "I'll give her the message."

"Thanks," Kimberly said as the door clicked shut.

Liza tried to begin her monologue again, but angry tears were blurring her vision. Didn't Kimberly and Faith realize how cruel they were being? Liza was good enough to carry a message about the party, but she wasn't good enough to be invited. It would serve Faith right if Liza never told her about the hot plate or the microwave or whatever it was. It would serve Faith right if the party turned out to be a disaster.

Of course, it wasn't completely realistic to expect an invitation from someone who wasn't speaking to you. Ever since Erin had given them a citation, Faith hadn't said a single word to Liza. She didn't even yell or complain anymore. She just floated in and out of the room as if Liza didn't exist.

It was driving Liza crazy! She'd tried everything to get Faith's attention. She'd thrown away all her candles. She'd written Faith a note of apology. She'd even tried talking to Erin to see about getting Faith's name off the citation.

Nothing had worked. Faith had shut Liza out completely. But Faith was going to be sorry, Liza was sure of that. Liza couldn't wait to see the expression on Faith's face when Liza returned from her callback with Lawrence Briscoe and announced that she had been cast as Lady Macbeth.

Liza knew in her gut she was going to get the part. Why else would Briscoe want to meet with her privately? Of course, he was meeting with a few other girls, too, but Liza was sure that none of them had—what was it Briscoe had said?—her depth and maturity. Liza felt a rush of adrenaline every time she thought about reading for Briscoe again. She was going to knock him off his feet.

So who cared about Faith's stupid party? It was the same night as Liza's callback anyway, so Liza couldn't have gone even if she'd wanted to.

A key turned in the lock, and Faith barged into the room, throwing her book bag on her bed. Without even looking at Liza, she unhooked the pearls she'd borrowed from Lauren, pulled off the white dress she'd borrowed from KC, and tossed them onto her bed.

Obviously, Faith's interview with Lawrence Briscoe hadn't gone too well. Faith was probably furious that Briscoe hadn't shown the same interest in her that he'd shown in Liza. Liza couldn't help smiling.

Dressed only in her underwear, Faith marched over to her dresser and started yanking out drawers, flinging clothes to the floor as she searched for something. Well, if Faith wanted to be rude and inconsiderate, Liza would do her one better. Liza would rub it in that she had a callback interview with Briscoe while Faith didn't.

"How was your interview?" Liza asked sweetly as Faith covered the floor in a blizzard of T-shirts, shorts, and socks.

"I don't want to talk about it."

Liza clucked sympathetically. "I wouldn't take it too personally if you didn't hit it off. There is a cultural difference, you know, and of course your average college freshman must seem very unsophisticated to someone like him."

Faith's hand paused in midair, still holding a pair of navy gym shorts. "What's that supposed to mean?"

Liza wandered over to her dresser and began

pulling a brush through her thick, fuzzy hair. "Oh, nothing."

"Are you calling me average?"

"Of course not!" Liza protested, smiling at Faith's reflection in her makeup mirror. "It's just that it's rare in someone our age to have the depth of a mature woman."

Faith's eyes took on a harsh gleam. "Where did you hear that?" she demanded, her reflection moving closer.

Liza turned around to face Faith. "Hear what?"

"That drivel about depth and maturity."

"It wasn't drivel," Liza sniffed, turning her back on Faith again. "Lawrence was merely paying me a well-deserved compliment."

Faith came around to Liza's right and blocked Liza's view of herself in the mirror. "Was that before or after he told you you had raw talent just waiting to burst forth, to be shaped by a knowing hand?"

Liza's mouth fell open. Had Faith been eavesdropping on her audition? Had she somehow bugged Briscoe's office? "You don't know what you're talking about," she said.

Faith moved back to her dresser and pulled a T-shirt out of her drawer. "Looks like I know a lot more about Briscoe than you do."

Faith was acting like such a know-it-all. Liza still couldn't figure out how Faith knew so much, unless Faith had come right out and asked Briscoe about Liza. That had to be it. Faith was angry that Briscoe had spent his time with her talking about Liza instead of her. Now that Liza finally understood, she could afford to be a little generous. She'd try to bolster Faith a little bit by talking about that stupid dinner Faith was throwing for Melissa and Brooks.

"Kimberly asked me to give you a message," Liza said, putting down the hairbrush. "She doesn't need a hot plate. Derek's got a friend off-campus with a kitchen. They're going to cook there tomorrow night."

"Thmmmph," Faith said in what was probably as close to "Thank you" as she was going to come. Then she reached into her drawer and pulled out a pair of candlesticks.

Liza gasped. She'd thought she'd thrown them all away when she cleaned out the room. But she'd stashed candlesticks all over when she first bought them. She must have forgotten about this pair.

"What are *these* doing here?" Faith asked accusingly. "Are you trying to get me in trouble again?"

"Oops!" Liza said. "I must have overlooked them."

"Overlooked them!" Faith shouted. "It looks

more as if you were trying to frame me."

"Now why would I try to do that?" Liza demanded. "I already told Erin the whole thing was my fault. What more can I do?"

"You don't want to hear my answer to that," Faith fumed, throwing the candlesticks on the floor.

"Hey!" Liza cried, stooping to pick them up. "Don't treat them that way. They're my tools. They help me find the character within myself."

"Come off it," Faith snapped, pulling a pair of denim shorts out of the drawer and slipping them on. "You are so pretentious."

"I am not!" Liza objected. "I'm just telling the truth. Of course, from your lowly viewpoint, the things I say may *sound* pretentious because they're so far above your head. You wouldn't know what it's like to be an up-and-coming star. You wouldn't know what it's like to be recognized by a world-famous director."

"Hah!" Faith said, kneeling down and scooping up her clothes from the floor.

"I don't care what you think of me anyway," Liza said. "As long as Lawrence Briscoe appreciates my talent, I don't need anybody else's approval. And I wouldn't go to your stupid dinner, either, even if you invited me, because I have *better* things to do. Lawrence has invited me to a special private session and he's going to cast me as Lady Macbeth."

Faith started laughing.

"What's your problem?" Liza demanded.

"Poor Liza," Faith said, shaking her head. "Poor, poor Liza."

Liza didn't like Faith's referring to her in the third person, and she certainly didn't like Faith's snobby, superior attitude. "Stop talking like that," she said.

Faith gave Liza a genuinely pitying look. "You still don't get it, do you?"

"Get what?"

"Briscoe."

"What about him?"

"The guy's a total lech! He's not interested in your talent."

"Of course he is. Why else would he ask me to come back for a private interview?"

Faith stood up and dumped her clothes in the open drawer. "Let me guess," she said. "He wants to find out if you have *passion for the theater.*"

Liza was shocked. How could Faith have known that, too? But it didn't really matter how Faith had found out. The point was, Faith was jealous. She couldn't stand the idea that Liza's theatrical career was advancing so quickly while her own was stalling.

"You have no idea how bitter you sound," Liza

said, putting down the candlesticks and turning to face Faith. "And how pathetic. You can't stand the idea that Lawrence saw something special in me and thinks *my* talent is worth developing. The only way you know how to get back at me is to make me feel bad about myself. Well, it's not working, Faith. I just feel sorry for you."

"You! Sorry for me?" Faith's eyes looked as if they were bugging out of her head. "Some sleazebag director drops the same lines on every innocent girl who walks into his office and you fall for it and you feel sorry for *me*?"

"That's what I said. Poor Faith," Liza mocked. "Poor, poor Faith. Maybe if she wasn't such a goody-goody and so uptight, she wouldn't feel threatened every time a man is nice to her. Ask Scott if you don't believe me."

"That has nothing to do—"

"Sure it does," Liza said, planting her hands on her hips. "You're so afraid of living, you automatically condemn anyone who isn't like you. Well, let me give you a little bit of insight into yourself. You're not a good judge of people. You don't know the first thing about people."

"And you do?" Faith yelled. "You're not exactly Miss Popularity."

Liza felt as if Faith had stuck a knife into her

stomach and twisted it around. That had to be the meanest, nastiest, most horrible thing anyone had ever said to her.

"Well, at least I know how to talk to men!" Liza screamed as tears welled up in her eyes again. "That's something you'll never learn. No wonder you're alone all the time. At the rate you're going, I'll bet you *never* have a boyfriend again!"

Grabbing her toiletry bag and her towel, Liza stomped out of the room so she could drown her tears in a long, hot shower.

Faith, too, felt on the verge of tears as the door banged shut. She couldn't believe how vicious they'd both been. But she didn't regret the brutal things she'd said to Liza. Every word was true. And long overdue.

Which raised a big question. What if every word Liza had said was also true? Maybe Faith *was* a goody-goody. And maybe she *was* uptight. But that was because it was too dangerous to be any other way. Even with her recent good behavior, she'd still gotten in trouble.

Maybe Liza was right about Briscoe, too. Faith hadn't been absolutely sure he was making a pass at her. She could have misinterpreted his friendliness as sleaziness. He really wasn't that much older than she was. And he hadn't said or done any one specific thing that she could point a finger at.

Faith sank onto her bed and curled up into a ball. She was starting to get a much clearer picture of herself, and she didn't like what she saw. She saw a girl who'd been so caught up in her personal problems that she'd just insulted a very important director. She saw a girl who'd been pushing away an adorable guy just because he didn't wear shoes all the time and didn't know his career path yet.

Maybe Faith had just been looking at everything the wrong way. Maybe she was just a fool who'd never have love or success in her life because she was too rigid. With so many maybes, the only thing Faith knew for sure was that she felt terrible.

This wasn't a new feeling. Faith had been feeling terrible ever since Tuesday, when she'd blamed Scott for the citation. She'd been having such a good time with him until she'd seen Erin's note on the door. And the dripping candles hadn't been his fault any more than they'd been her fault. So why had she yelled at him that way? To hurt him just because she felt hurt? She owed him an apology.

Faith picked up the phone receiver and dialed Scott's number. As she heard the line ring she started to panic and almost hung up, but then she heard Scott's friendly voice.

"Springfield House of Detention," he answered.

"You fail 'em, we jail 'em."

"Uh. . . hi, Scott," Faith began timidly. "This is Faith." She waited for the click as he hung up on her, but all she heard was silence. "Are you still there?" she asked.

"I'm here." Scott didn't sound so cheerful anymore.

Faith hugged her pillow to her chest. "I . . . well, I know you're probably really mad at me for the way I acted the other day, and I really don't blame you one bit, but I just wanted to say I'm sorry."

Scott said nothing.

"Are you still there?" Faith asked.

"Yeah, I'm here."

"So . . . do you want to say anything?"

"Well," Scott said, "I'm just really surprised. I didn't expect to hear from you again."

"I know," Faith said. "That's my fault, too. I really overreacted when I got that citation. I hope you can forgive me."

"Well, sure I forgive you," Scott said. "I forgave you right away. I know how scared you were about that peer review thing."

What a generous soul Scott was. How many other people would be that understanding while someone was yelling at them? Maybe Faith had been an even bigger fool than she'd thought to push him away.

"Well," Scott said, "it was really nice of you to call."

"Yeah. . ." Faith said. She didn't know what to say next, but she didn't want to hang up.

"So, I guess you're really busy planning your big dinner," Scott said.

Faith was encouraged. At least he was interested in keeping the conversation going. And maybe he was even giving her an opening. "Yeah," she said. "There's still a lot to do."

"But you've got all your friends to help you," Scott said. "That should make it easier."

Faith still couldn't tell if Scott was hinting or not, but she decided to take a chance. She might live to regret it, but she certainly wouldn't feel any worse about herself than she did already.

"Actually," Faith said, "I could still use some more help. That is, if you know anyone with restaurant experience."

"I might be able to think of someone," Scott said. Faith could almost hear him smiling. "The party's Sunday at six," she told him. "Why don't you come by around five o'clock."

"Cool. I'll be there. See ya."

After Faith hung up, she stared at the phone, feeling just as insecure and indecisive as she had before she'd called. Had she just made a big mistake? What if Scott never showed up? Or, even worse, what if Scott *did* show up and did something wild and unexpected? Things were going to be hard enough for Melissa and Brooks without Scott's making them even worse.

"What have I done?" Faith groaned aloud. "What have I done?"

Twelve

"I knew Scott wouldn't show up," Faith said as she and Lauren grabbed opposite ends of a white linen tablecloth and shook it several times to get the creases out. They stood in the rec center reception room, which Faith had reserved for the engagement dinner. "I should have known better than to ask him for help. He'll just let me down again."

"What time was he supposed to get here?" Lauren asked as they let the tablecloth flutter down onto the table.

"Five o'clock."

"It's only one minute after five," Lauren said.

"Give him a chance." Her wispy light brown hair was damp and sticking to the back of her neck, and her glasses kept sliding down her nose.

Faith blamed herself for the heat in the room. She should have thought to set up some fans so her guests wouldn't liquefy, but she'd had so many other things on her mind she'd forgotten. Why hadn't she written it down on one of her lists? And why hadn't she made another list of all the reasons why she shouldn't trust Scott?

Faith plugged in her portable electric iron and sprayed the tablecloth with a mist of water. "That's the problem," she said. "I've given him too many chances already. I should have learned my lesson by now." Faith ran the iron over the creases that were still in the tablecloth.

Lauren took a stack of white linen napkins and began folding them. "Even if he doesn't show, and he still might, you shouldn't blame yourself. I know you've got your Mr. Right checklist and all, but that doesn't give you complete control over the guys you date."

Faith smiled at her former roommate. What a good friend she was. Considerate and caring and supportive. Why did Lauren ever have to leave and sell her dorm contract to Liza?

Well, at least Liza wouldn't be around to bother

her tonight, Faith thought as she ran the iron over the crisscrossing folds in the material. That was one less thing to worry about. There was too much on her mind now, as it was. They didn't have enough serving pieces, and the refrigerator in the pantry next to the conference room was on the blink, which meant the salad leaves were going to wilt. Faith had already sent Derek to go buy some ice at the supermarket so they could at least keep the refrigerator lukewarm.

"Chairs!" Barney Sharfenburger announced as he entered the reception room, three wooden folding chairs hanging on each of his powerful arms. Barney, Brooks's roommate, was a body builder, but the effect of his massive muscles was offset by the fact that he had a crew cut and black horn-rimmed glasses. "Where shall I set 'em up?"

"Three on each side," Faith directed as she turned off the iron and unplugged it. "We're going for the restaurant effect."

"Faith!" Kimberly called from the pantry. "We have another problem."

"Could you help Barney?" Faith asked Lauren as she ran across the carpeted reception room to the pantry.

Kimberly stood at a counter, dressed in a white blouse and black pants, like everyone else helping out. Uniforms had been Faith's idea, to make it seem more like a real restaurant. Kimberly was staring down at the open white cardboard box that contained the cake Faith had ordered.

"Look," Kimberly said, sliding the box toward Faith.

At first, Faith didn't notice anything wrong. Then she caught it. As she'd requested, "Congratulations Mellissa and Brooks" was written in graceful pink sugar script, but the baker had added an extra *l* to Melissa's name. The icing, too, was beginning to look shiny and soft from the lack of refrigeration.

"What should we do?" Kimberly asked.

I won't panic, Faith told herself for the tenth time that hour. This party had to go well. Melissa's future happiness with Brooks depended on it. And they'd all worked so hard. If it fell apart now, Faith was afraid *she'd* fall apart. It was the only thing she'd done lately that she felt proud of. She certainly wasn't proud of her taste in men, no matter how much Lauren tried to convince her it wasn't her fault. It was five after five already, and there was still no sign of Scott.

"Watch this," Faith said, taking a plastic knife and surgically removing the second *l*. Then she blended the remaining letters together.

"Brilliant," Kimberly complimented her.

"Make way for the ice," shouted Derek as he came flying toward the refrigerator with two giant dripping bags of ice cubes. Tall and skinny, with a close-cropped afro, he wore oversized glasses that magnified his brown eyes.

Kimberly opened the refrigerator door just in time for Derek to throw the bags inside. "Looks more like water," she joked.

Derek took an ice cube from the bag and touched it to Kimberly's skin. "You tell me, physicist," he said as Kimberly squealed. "Is this H_2O in its liquid or solid state?"

"Grow up," Kimberly cried as she tried to wriggle away from Derek and the ice cube. "Remember. This is an *engagement* dinner, not one of your demonstrations for schoolchildren."

Derek's face grew sober, and he tossed the ice cube into the pantry sink. "Engagement dinner," he echoed. "Doesn't that sound weird?"

"What's weird about it?" Faith asked. "People get engaged all the time. It's natural to celebrate."

"I think I know what Derek means, though," Kimberly said. "It's the idea of getting married at *our* age."

Faith shrugged. "Somebody's got to be the first." And at the rate she was going, it certainly wasn't going to be her. Not that she wanted to be married.

She was still much too young. She did like the idea, though, of having a secure relationship with someone she could depend on. Someone who'd show up when he'd promised to. But Faith felt selfish thinking about Scott and her other problems. Today was Melissa's and Brooks's day.

"Sorry we're late," KC called as she and Courtney Conner entered the pantry from the hall. Each of them carried a heavy wooden chest, which they deposited on the counter.

"Here's some of the Tri Beta china and silverware," said Courtney, the attractive blond president of the sorority. Now that KC was a member of Tri Beta, the two of them were good friends.

"We'll take extra good care of it," Faith promised as Courtney and KC unloaded the gold-rimmed plates and engraved silverware with a pattern of tiny bows and ribbons.

"This stuff is gorgeous," Kimberly marveled as she helped Faith unpack and dust everything off. "Melissa and Brooks are going to have the most elegant 'restaurant' in the world for their special dinner."

"Bonsoir mesdames et messieurs!" called a cheerful male voice with a dubious French accent.

Faith turned and saw Scott bounce into the room, dressed for the occasion in basketball shorts, a football jersey, and a cropped white jacket. He even carried a paper napkin over his arm.

Faith didn't know whether to laugh at his outfit or yell at herself. She'd been so convinced he wouldn't show up that she'd never considered the possibility that he might simply be late. Now Faith felt foolish for underestimating him.

"That's some outfit," Faith said. "Who are you supposed to be, a French waiter?"

"Oui, oui, mademoiselle," Scott said, bowing low so that his shaggy blond hair flipped upside down. Then he popped up and winked. "I saved this from my waitering days in high school. I figured I could serve the dinner if you didn't already have someone."

Faith covered her mouth with her hand. She'd completely forgotten. Even with all her careful planning, she'd left out one very important job: waiter. Everyone else was going to be busy with their own assignments, including Faith. Scott was the only one who was available. And he was the only one with a waiter's jacket.

"I guess you've got the job," Faith said.

Scott grinned broadly. "Thanks, boss." He grabbed Faith and spun her around, nearly knocking the stack of Tri Beta china plates from the table.

Faith's heart almost stopped short. What had she just gotten herself into?

✱ ✱ ✱

"Those are beautiful, Win," KC said a few minutes later as Winnie carefully unpacked the cream-colored place cards.

Winnie double-checked the folded cards to make sure she hadn't forgotten any. Each name was written in italic letters and had a decorative rosebud in the top right corner. The rosebud design had been repeated, many times larger, as a border on a giant sign that Josh was now tacking to the wall of the room. The sign said: MELISSA AND BROOKS.

Winnie was very pleased with the way their decorations had turned out. They'd done it all on the computer, except for the pink and green Winnie had added to the roses afterward. Winnie had also bought two dozen real pink roses, which she was going to arrange as a centerpiece for the table.

It was all so romantic. And just one more instance of Winnie living through someone else's relationship. But that was about to change. Place cards and roses weren't the only things Winnie had brought with her today. Winnie had come armed with the weapon that was going to put the stars back in Josh's eyes.

Josh still had his back to her as he pushed thumbtacks into the sign. Sneaking up behind him, she took another thumbtack from the plastic box on the table and tacked a glossy travel brochure on the wall next to the sign. The cover, the most colorful Winnie could find at the three travel agencies she'd visited in the past few days, featured Paris—the Eiffel Tower, the Louvre museum, and Notre Dame cathedral.

Winnie peeked around so she could see the reaction on Josh's face. Would he seem shocked? Disappointed? Angry?

Josh whistled a tuneless little tune and cocked his head to one side as he stared up at the MELISSA AND BROOKS sign. "You think the sign's even?" he asked Winnie as he stepped back a few feet. "Or is it higher on the right?"

He hadn't even noticed the brochures! His brown eyes had that same glazed-over, absorbed look they had when he was hypnotized by his computer screen. Winnie felt like screaming. What did she have to do to get his attention?

"It's fine," Winnie assured him, pulling the brochure from the wall and waving it in front of his face.

"What's that?" KC asked as she wiped off the china plates with a paper towel and set them at the table.

Now why couldn't Josh have asked that question?

"It's helping me decide where I'm going to study," Winnie said. "Of course, Paris has the Sorbonne, and so many cultural opportunities, but I've already spent so much time there. I thought I might choose Nice this time."

There. That ought to do it. Any second, Josh's face would get back that alert look she used to see so often. The glaze in his eyes would clear and his face would take on that pained, intense expression that Peter wore all the time now.

Josh still looked half asleep. "You going somewhere?" he asked, tugging absently on a wisp of brown hair, his eyes never leaving the sign.

"Yeah," Winnie said, trying to control her frustration. "I really fell in love with France last summer when I was there. I haven't been able to stop thinking about it since then. I think that's where I belong."

"What?" KC asked, again showing more reaction than Josh. "You're going to Europe, too?"

"I've been giving it some serious thought," Winnie answered.

Josh took the brochure from Winnie's hand and started reading it, but he didn't seem surprised or upset.

"Well?" Winnie finally asked him, unable to take it any longer. "What do you think of my leaving? I might be gone for a long, *long* time. That means we wouldn't see each other."

Josh didn't answer. He seemed more interested in the brochure than in what she was saying.

"Josh!" Winnie cried. "Are you listening to me? Or am I talking to a wall? How would you feel if I went to Europe? Would you miss me?"

"Of course not," Josh said, looking up.

Winnie stared at him in shock. "What?"

"I'd go with you," Josh said matter-of-factly. "They have computers in France, too, you know." Ruffling Winnie's hair affectionately, Josh turned his attention back to the sign. "So what do you think? Is it too high on the right?"

"Let me see that brochure," KC said.

Winnie felt as if she were going to explode. While it was nice to know Josh would follow her wherever she went, a pat on the head wasn't the response she'd been hoping for. Was that all she was to him—a puppy dog? A constant companion, but underfoot, taken for granted, and practically ignored? What had happened to pulling each other close and sharing fevered, urgent kisses?

The intensity was all gone. And it looked as if it was never coming back.

Thirteen

"**B**rooks!" his stepmother cooed half an hour later as they entered the rec center reception room. "This is lovely! Did you kids do this yourselves?"

Brooks couldn't answer right away. He was too amazed by what he saw. The small carpeted room looked like an elegant restaurant. The central table was covered with a white linen cloth. China plates with gold borders were placed among gleaming silverware. A tall crystal vase filled with pink roses sat in the middle of the table, with brass candelabra on either side. The recessed lights in the ceiling had been turned down low, and the lighted candles flickered, casting a golden glow about the room.

"This is nicer than the restaurant I was going to take you to," said Brooks's father, shoving his hands into the pockets of his beige linen pants and taking it all in.

Forty years old, Fred Baldwin was of medium height, about the same height as Brooks, though his build was leaner from the marathons he ran. His face was weather beaten and tan from weekends spent on the golf course, and his grizzled hair was still thick and curly.

Sue, Brooks's stepmom, moved close to her husband and slipped her arm around his waist. Unlike her husband's, her skin was pale and unlined, making her look younger than forty. She wasn't pretty, but she had an interesting, friendly face, with wide-set brown eyes, a strong nose, and a square jaw. Her shoulder-length hair was dark and wavy, and she wore a sleeveless red linen dress with a gold chain belt and a simple gold cuff bracelet on one arm.

"This is making me feel positively ancient," Sue said to her husband. "Imagine—us, old enough to have a son who's getting married."

"Well, he did speed things up a little," Mr. Baldwin said, with a sideways glance at Brooks.

While Brooks's parents had been surprised and a little upset when Brooks told them he was engaged, they hadn't tried to talk him out of it. They'd just explained how things were going to be more difficult—like working to pay for married students' housing while going to school. They'd warned him, too, that either he or Melissa might have to compromise on their choice of grad school in order to stay together. Both of his parents liked Melissa, though, and approved of her intelligence and ambition.

"So where are the McDormands?" Sue asked. "I'm dying to meet them and see Melissa again."

"They should be here any minute," Brooks said, though he was just guessing. He hadn't seen Melissa or spoken to her since after the meeting about the party. He'd tried, of course, to reach her, but she was never in her room, and she hadn't gone out of her way to find him, either.

Brooks felt bad that they'd never had a chance to smooth things over before tonight, but he wasn't seriously worried. They were probably both just tense about their parents' meeting each other. This was a big step. This made the whole idea of marriage so much more real. But once everyone said hello tonight, the ice would be broken and they'd all feel more comfortable.

"No, Ma, that's not the right door," Melissa's voice called in the hall outside. "It's over here."

Brooks heard a woman's voice mumble something, then Melissa appeared in the doorway to the reception room. She looked summery and neat in a navy skirt and short sleeve white blouse. Her copper hair was pulled back in a tortoiseshell headband.

"Are we late?" she asked tensely, as her parents appeared behind her.

Mrs. McDormand looked pudgy, in a yellow dress with white polka dots that seemed a little too tight. Over the dress, she wore a navy blue blazer with a plastic purple flower pinned to the lapel. Her brownish gray hair had rigid, roller-shaped curls framing her face.

Mr. McDormand, hovering in the hall behind his wife and his daughter, kept looking around nervously as if any minute someone he knew might appear from around a corner. He was tall and cadaverously thin, with a bald spot in the middle of his red hair. His face was slightly puffy, but he was clean shaven and looked freshly washed. He wore a plain white shirt and a pair of tan pants with a brown stripe down the side of each leg. Brooks wondered if those were the pants he used to wear when he was a doorman at the Springfield Hotel.

"Melissa!" Sue Baldwin greeted Melissa, walking toward her with open arms. "Come give me a hug, daughter-in-law."

Brooks loved the way Sue always referred to him

as her son, not her stepson, and he was glad she was treating Melissa the same way. Sue was so warm and affectionate she'd make Melissa relax right away.

"How are you, Mrs. Baldwin?" Melissa said stiffly, patting Sue's back as they embraced.

"Please call us Fred and Sue," Brooks's father said, striding forward to shake Melissa's hand. Then he held out his hand to Melissa's mother. "Fred Baldwin," he said as Mrs. McDormand weakly returned the handshake. "It's a pleasure."

"Yes," Mrs. McDormand said, though she looked more anxious than pleased.

"Fred Baldwin," repeated Brooks's father, reaching past everyone to shake Mr. McDormand's hand.

Mr. McDormand mumbled something and looked bewildered. Melissa looked as if she'd rather be someplace else. So far this wasn't going too well. Maybe it was time for Brooks to step in and help things along.

"I'm very glad to meet Melissa's parents," Brooks said to the McDormands as he put his arm around Melissa. "It's wonderful to have you share this special night with us."

"We were happy to be invited," Mrs. McDormand said, giving Melissa a look that Brooks didn't understand.

"Well, shall we sit down?" Brooks suggested.

"Melissa and her friends have put together a big gourmet meal, and I'm starving."

"Why don't you sit next to me so we can gab," Sue said to Mrs. McDormand. "You can tell me all sorts of cute stories about Melissa when she was a baby."

Melissa didn't look too pleased with that idea. She turned to her father. "Why don't you sit next to me?" she suggested.

Brooks's father took a seat on the other side of Mr. McDormand. "So tell me. . ." He paused, realizing he didn't know Mr. McDormand's first name.

"Jim," Mr. McDormand replied. His voice was so soft that Brooks, now sitting opposite Melissa, could barely hear him.

"Jim," echoed Mr. Baldwin in his deep, confident voice. "What line of work are you in?"

Mr. McDormand didn't answer right away, and Melissa sat up straight. "My dad's taking a little time off right now," she said. "He hasn't been feeling too well." Her voice cracked on the last word, and she coughed to cover it up.

Brooks wanted to reach across the table, to grab her hand and let her know there was no reason to get so defensive. Even if his parents knew the truth about her father, they wouldn't hold it against her. They wouldn't hold it against her father, either. But Brooks had a feeling his father was beginning to sense that he and Mr. McDormand didn't have much in common.

"So do you work?" Sue asked Mrs. McDormand.

"I'm a housekeeper," Mrs. McDormand said simply.

Sue betrayed no reaction. "That must be hard," she said. "I don't think people appreciate how difficult housework is."

Mrs. McDormand showed Sue her roughened hands. "Twenty years takes its toll."

Brooks noticed Sue slid her own smooth, manicured hands beneath the table so they wouldn't contrast too strongly with Mrs. McDormand's. Melissa, who still hadn't said a word to Brooks since she'd arrived, looked as if she wanted to slide beneath the table, too.

"The first course will be served in approximately five minutes," Faith announced, poking her head out a side door.

"Faith!" Sue called to Brooks's ex-girlfriend in pleasure and surprise. "What are you doing here?"

"Just helping out some good friends," Faith said with a smile. "It's nice to see you again." She ducked behind the door and Brooks heard the clatter of dishes inside.

"Isn't it lovely that you're still friends," Sue said to Brooks. She turned to Mrs. McDormand. "Brooks and Faith. . ." She stopped midsentence.

Brooks knew she'd changed her mind about telling Melissa's mother that Brooks and Faith had dated for four years. It didn't exactly seem necessary at a time like this.

There was more silence. Mrs. McDormand stared at her empty plate, and Mr. McDormand stared into space.

"I know what we can do to pass the time," Sue said. "We can open presents."

"Presents?" said several people at once.

Brooks said it because he hadn't seen his parents walk in with any boxes.

Melissa said it because she was surprised to receive anything at all.

Mrs. McDormand said it with a shocked and horrified look on her face. "I'm sorry," she stammered. "I didn't know we were supposed to bring something."

"You weren't," said Brooks's father smoothly, reaching into the inside pocket of his beige linen jacket. "This is just a Baldwin family tradition." He pulled out a white envelope and two slim velvet boxes.

As the McDormands watched with glum faces, Mr. Baldwin handed one of the boxes to Melissa.

"I really can't accept this," Melissa protested, but Sue hushed her.

"I spent an entire afternoon picking it out," Sue said. "I'll be heartbroken if you don't take it."

Reluctantly Melissa opened the box, and her mouth fell open. Then she turned the box around so everyone could see a gold bracelet with colorful semiprecious stones.

"It's very pretty," Mrs. McDormand said in a tight voice.

"Your turn," Mr. Baldwin said, handing Brooks a similar box.

Brooks opened it and started grinning. Years ago, when he'd admired his father's stainless steel and gold diving watch, his father had promised to get him one just like it when he became a man. Apparently, Brooks had grown up.

"You're the best, Dad," he said, standing up and reaching across the table to shake his father's hand.

Mr. Baldwin handed Brooks the envelope. "Why don't you open this later," he suggested.

Brooks knew exactly what was in the envelope and why his father didn't want him to open it in front of everyone. It was a check. Probably for five hundred or a thousand dollars. On top of the Baldwins' other expensive gifts, the check would only make the McDormands feel even more embarrassed that they had come empty-handed.

"I have something for you two at home," Mrs. McDormand promised. "I'll give it to you the next time I see you."

Brooks strongly suspected Melissa's mother was lying, and felt bad that his parents' extravagance had put the McDormonds in an awkward position.

He was beginning to feel bad, too, that his parents were so young and attractive. The McDormands, while probably about the same age, looked almost old enough to be *their* parents. And it almost seemed unfair that his parents were so much more affluent and sophisticated. How could Melissa's parents feel anything but inadequate by comparison?

Brooks had been sure their parents would like each other, even if they were from vastly different backgrounds. They were all nice people. And they had to get along if they were going to be in-laws. But from the way things were going, they were going to run out of things to talk about before the first course was over.

KC and Winnie appeared with water pitchers and six bowls of chilled cucumber soup on a tray.

"Would you like some water, Mr. McDormand?" KC asked. Brooks thought he heard her place special emphasis on the word *water*. Was that because Mr. McDormand was an alcoholic? Maybe Melissa wanted her father to stay sober tonight, and her friends were helping her.

After KC and Winnie filled everyone's glasses, they returned to the kitchen, and the room was quiet again.

"Good soup," Mr. McDormand said a few minutes later, in his sole effort to break the silence.

"Delicious," Sue agreed.

The next words were spoken by Scott when he came to clear the empty bowls. "Having a good time, folks?"

"Wonderful," Mr. Baldwin said, a little too heartily.

The main course was a tasty breast of chicken with some vegetables Brooks didn't recognize and brown rice. Brooks forced himself to try everything so it wouldn't be too obvious that he'd lost his appetite. Things were bad enough without his putting more of a damper on the evening.

When Winnie, KC, and Scott came out of the kitchen to clear the dishes, Sue leaned down and started fumbling with her oversize purse. Then she sat up and smiled.

"We have one more surprise for you," she said, pulling something out of her large shoulder bag. "Since our two families are about to be joined, I think we should celebrate with a toast. I bought an insulated bottle of Moet champagne when we got to Springfield. It should still be nice and chilled."

Melissa's eyes widened in shock, but Sue didn't notice. Brooks did, though. He knew why she'd suddenly grabbed the edge of the table as if she were afraid her chair was going to go flying through the air. He knew her head was swiveling back and forth as she looked from her father to her mother.

Brooks stole a look at Mr. McDormand. He'd been fine so far tonight, but that was because KC and Winnie kept him waterlogged. Now, he was staring at the bottle with a tense look on his face.

"Then, afterward," Sue continued, "I thought it might be nice if we old folks went out on the town and got to know each other better. I've heard there's a great nightclub called The Magic Act where the bartender makes some wicked margaritas."

Melissa's face literally turned green. She looked at her father with panic-stricken eyes. Brooks knew he should step in here, but his mind was a total blank.

Sue handed the champagne bottle to Scott. "Would you open this for us, please?"

As Scott took the bottle into the kitchen, Sue reached into her bag again and pulled out a package of plastic champagne glasses. "I came prepared, didn't I?" She laughed at herself. Then she opened the package and started passing out the glasses.

Brooks watched helplessly as she put a champagne glass in front of Mr. McDormand.

"Mi, mi, mi, mi, mi, mi, mi, mi, mi." Liza warmed up her voice with a musical scale and watched herself in the mirror at the same time. She wanted to see exactly what Lawrence Briscoe was going to see when she went to her callback interview in a few minutes. She wanted to hone her every inflection, her every gesture, so Briscoe would be blown away by her performance.

Liza smoothed a tiny wrinkle in her burgundy dress, the same dress she'd worn for her first audition. Low-cut in front, but not *too* low, and tapered to flatter her generous figure, it made her look older. Queenlike. Besides, the dress had brought her luck before. Hopefully, her luck would hold until Briscoe cast her as Lady Macbeth.

No. It would be more than luck. It would be her God-given talent, which had finally been recognized. It would be her unmistakable aura of stardom, the kind she could feel every time she'd passed a celebrity on the streets of Manhattan. Liza had it, too. She was sure of it. And soon *she* would be the celebrity walking down the sidewalk while some would-be hopeful looked on enviously.

"You're *going* to get that part," Liza told herself in a fierce voice. "He likes you. He told you so."

Yes, but how much? asked a nagging voice inside her that sounded annoyingly like Faith. *And in what way?*

Briscoe *couldn't* have called her back just because

he was interested in her body. Could he? Briscoe was a complete professional. One had only to see his production of *A Midsummer Night's Dream* to know that.

Of course, it did sound just the slightest bit suspicious that he'd asked her to meet him at night, alone in that cozy little room with the big couch. And "passion for the theater" was an odd choice of words. Especially since he'd said the same exact thing to Faith. Now that Liza had had some time to think about what Faith had said, she'd realized Briscoe must have used the same lines on both of them. That was the only possible way Faith could have known everything Briscoe had said to her. The question was, how many other girls had he said it to? How many other girls was he planning to charm into lying down on his casting couch?

No! That couldn't be it! Briscoe was going to discover her. Make her a star. Liza shuddered at the words. They had to be the oldest cliché in the theater. Had Briscoe really played her for the fool? Was he already laughing at her gullibility, the way everyone else laughed at her hair, her makeup, and her brassy voice? Was he just waiting to see how much more of a fool she'd make of herself, just to get a part?

She wasn't a fool. She was a serious actress with depth and maturity. Hadn't he said that? Or was it just another line she'd been too stupid to pick up on? He'd acted as if he liked her, respected her. But so had a lot of other people, and they'd all ended up deserting her or making fun of her or both.

Liza looked at herself in the mirror again.

She saw Lady Macbeth.

She saw an overweight freshman with badly dyed hair who was totally deluded about herself.

She saw a future star.

She saw a stupid kid whose nose was starting to run because she was crying in confusion and frustration.

She saw a girl who was about to embark on the most exciting adventure of her life.

She saw a girl who was going to do the smart thing and avoid Briscoe-the-creep like the plague.

Collapsing on her bed, Liza sobbed into her pillow and beat the mattress in frustration. She didn't know who she was anymore. The only thing she did know was that her big break wasn't going to happen tonight. She wasn't going to meet with Briscoe.

Fourteen

She brought *what*?" Faith cried as Scott showed her the bottle of champagne. "How could she do something like that? She'll ruin everything." Faith grabbed the bottle and held it far away from her body, as if it were a time bomb about to explode.

"I guess no one told her about Mr. McDormand's problem, Scott said, leaning casually against the pantry counter.

While Faith was very grateful that Scott had brought the bottle directly to her rather than open it immediately outside, she found it very annoying that he was taking this so calmly. Didn't he understand what a disaster this was? After all her careful planning, after she had sent Winnie and KC out to the dining room every five minutes to keep an eye on Melissa's father, the whole thing was going to blow up in her face.

"What should we do?" Faith said. She put the bottle down on the counter and paced back and forth in front of it. KC and Winnie, who'd been clearing the dishes from the reception room, crowded into the tiny pantry with Faith and Scott.

"Mrs. Baldwin's asking for the bottle," Winnie said, her brown eyes wide with anxiety. "What are you going to tell her?"

"I don't know! I don't know!" Faith cried, her mind going numb with panic.

"I guess she won't believe us if we tell her we lost it?" KC suggested halfheartedly.

"No chance," Faith said, picking the bottle up again and reading the label, as if the answer to their problem might somehow be written on it.

She felt like dropping the bottle on the floor, but she didn't dare. A bottle like this had to cost fifty dollars, at least. If she broke it, she'd upset the Baldwins. But maybe that wasn't as bad as getting Mr. McDormand drunk.

Taking a deep breath, Faith started to raise the bottle above her head.

"Hi, folks," Sue said cheerfully, poking her head around the swinging door. "Everything all right in here?"

Faith guiltily lowered the bottle. "Just fine!" she chirped.

"I didn't hear the cork pop yet," Sue said. "We've got some thirsty people out here."

You don't know how thirsty, Faith thought.

Sue reached out for the bottle. "I can open it myself if you're busy getting dessert."

There was nothing Faith could do now. She was trapped.

"Non non, madame," Scott said in his fake French accent. "I wouldn't hear of it. This is a full-service restaurant. We do everything for you." Grabbing the bottle from Faith, he held the door open so Sue could walk out ahead of him.

Faith gave Scott an anguished look. What was he doing? Didn't he realize how serious this situation was? Or was he incapable of taking anything seriously?

Trust me, Scott mouthed as he disappeared through the doorway.

Faith couldn't just wait behind the door. She had to see what Scott was doing. Pushing the door open a crack, Faith peeped out. Winnie knelt on the floor so she could see from underneath Faith, and KC stood on tiptoe so she could watch from above.

With a deft motion, Scott peeled off the foil around the top of the bottle and rapidly twisted the cork. Melissa sat rigid in her chair, her face stony. The Baldwins smiled in anticipation, and the McDormands looked uncomfortable.

Pop! It sounded as if a gun had gone off as the cork flew out of the bottle and hit the ceiling. At the same moment, Faith's heart leaped in her chest. Any second now, Scott would begin to pour. Then it would be all over.

Scott tilted the bottle over Melissa's glass. But before a single drop had emerged, he screwed up his face and wrinkled his nose. He tilted the bottle back upright.

"What's the matter?" asked Sue.

Scott's expression became grim. He sniffed the air. He made a face. He raised the bottle to his nose and smelled it.

What was he doing? Faith exchanged a confused look with Winnie and KC.

Scott lowered the bottle and cleared his throat. "I'm terribly sorry," he said to Sue, his voice grave, "but there's something wrong with this champagne."

"But that's impossible," Mr. Baldwin cried. "We bought this from a very reputable dealer."

"I'm sure it's not the dealer's fault," Scott said,

tucking the bottle under his arm where no one could get at it. "It must have happened at the vineyard. Don't feel bad. This isn't the first time I've seen this happen. When I was a waiter at Le Cirque, it happened three or four times a year."

Faith couldn't believe Scott was lying so smoothly. He'd never worked at a four-star restaurant. But judging from the looks on the Baldwins' faces, they were buying it.

"It might not be a total loss," Scott said. "Let me take this back to the pantry and check. I'll be right back."

Faith, Winnie, and KC scurried back from the door just as Scott came barging through it.

Before Faith could thank Scott for saving the day, she heard Sue's voice right outside.

"Scott!" called Sue. "I'd like to smell that champagne."

"Get rid of it," Scott said, shoving the bottle into Faith's hand. "I'll cover for you."

Faith looked at the bottle as if it were poison. The last thing she'd intended to do was get near a bottle of alcohol, especially on school property. But there was no time to think about how this didn't fit into her plan. She had to get rid of the bottle before Sue grabbed it from her.

Oh please let me find a trash can before someone sees

me with this thing, Faith prayed as she dashed out into the hallway. She'd been hot before, but panic raised her body temperature at least another ten degrees.

Faith ran down the hallway, careening from right to left, as she searched for a trash can, an empty box, a recycling bin—any sort of receptacle large enough to hold a bottle. She didn't know the building too well, since she'd been in it only when she'd come for her *Macbeth* interview. The halls were spotless and empty—just her luck. Maybe she could find a ladies room or a janitor's closet.

One by one, Faith tried the doors along the corridor, but they were all locked. Was this some sort of cruel joke? A trash can shouldn't be so hard to find. Faith rounded the corner with so much force that she skidded on the floor and nearly collided with the wall.

Then, suddenly, she froze in horror. Heading straight toward her was the last person she wanted to see while holding a bottle of alcohol. Dressed in a black crepe dress and sauntering forward in two-inch heels was Faith's Resident Adviser, Erin Grant.

Faith wanted to turn and run, but Erin had already seen her. Faith was caught. The rest of her life was already written.

First Erin would whip out her official notepad and write a citation for a major infraction of dorm rules.

Then Faith would burst into tears and have to call her parents and tell them the responsible daughter they'd always been so proud of was about to get kicked out of school. Faith could almost hear the shocked silence on the other end of the line as her parents tried to fathom what had happened. Then Faith would go before the peer review board and get formal notice of her expulsion. She'd go back to her room and start packing while Liza looked on in glee, happy that she'd have the room to herself. Maybe that was what Liza had had in mind all along. Maybe Liza had broken the dorm rules on purpose, just to get rid of Faith. What did Liza care if Faith's entire future was destroyed? Faith would probably spend the rest of her life in hokey old Jacksonville, waiting tables or working at the five and dime, dreaming of the life she could have had.

Erin was only a few feet away now. Faith stared at her like a deer mesmerized by oncoming headlights. Erin stopped walking and looked from Faith to the bottle, back to Faith again. Her icy blue eyes narrowed, and she started to smile.

As Faith continued to stare helplessly, she realized that this girl didn't have an ounce of pity or human kindness. *Just make it quick,* Faith prayed. *Let's get it over with.*

Erin opened her mouth to say something, but the

squeak of a door opening stopped her and a pink flush crept into her dead-white face as she stared at something behind Faith.

Faith turned around and nearly dropped the champagne bottle in surprise. Lawrence Briscoe stood in the doorway of a nearby room, a smirk on his face.

Now it was Erin's turn to look like a deer caught in headlights. What was Erin so nervous about? Erin never looked anything but coolly in control. So what was going on?

The leer on Briscoe's face, the same one that had made Faith so nervous and uncomfortable when she'd had her interview, answered Faith's question. Erin was no doubt here to see Briscoe so they could "discuss," in private, Erin's "passion for theater." Faith looked at her watch. Wasn't Liza supposed to be meeting Briscoe now? Had Liza chickened out?

But none of this really mattered anymore. Faith would be leaving U. of S. any day now, and all this would just be a dim memory.

"Hullo, Faith," said Briscoe pleasantly.

Faith was surprised Briscoe even remembered her name. He must have interviewed at least a hundred people. But then Faith thought back to their conversation. How many interviewees had told Briscoe they were on probation and would get expelled if they were caught with alcohol? That was probably why Briscoe had made a pass at her in the first place.

"Do you two girls know each other?" Briscoe asked, glancing from one to the other.

"We live in the same dorm," Erin said, recovering some of her composure. "I'm her Resident Adviser."

"What does that mean, exactly?" Briscoe asked. "I'm not familiar with the term."

"It means I'm responsible for discipline," Erin said, staring at Faith's bottle again.

Briscoe's eyes seemed to take on an unearthly gleam. "I see," he said, and Faith had a feeling he really did understand. He turned his attention back to her. "Faith, love," Briscoe went on, holding out his hand. "Thanks so much for bringing me the prop. It will make our rehearsal go so much better."

Faith just stood there. She didn't have the slightest idea what Briscoe was talking about.

Briscoe walked toward her and took the champagne bottle out of Faith's hand. "This is exactly the kind I needed," he said as he returned to the doorway. "Very resourceful of you to find it for me."

Erin's smooth brow furrowed, and Faith finally realized what Briscoe had done. He'd covered for her! Now Erin wouldn't be able to give Faith a citation.

"Won't you come in?" Briscoe asked Erin politely, stepping aside so she could enter his lair. He closed the door behind them.

Even though Faith couldn't see them anymore, she could imagine him licking his lips and rubbing his hands together as he prepared to pounce on his victim. Then that dark picture was replaced by a much brighter one. Briscoe had saved her! Thanks to him, she wouldn't get kicked out of school after all. Maybe Briscoe wasn't so rotten after all.

The door opened again, and Briscoe poked his head out. Silently, he motioned for Faith to approach him.

Faith took a few steps forward. "Yes?" she whispered.

"You owe me," Briscoe said in a low, insinuating voice. "You will work on my *Macbeth* crew, and I will collect."

Fifteen

*J*ust one more lap, Melissa told herself Monday afternoon as she rounded the curve of the U. of S. outdoor track. She was running in the middle of the pack, well behind her usual first or second place, and her thighs were burning with pain. But after nearly an entire day of running around and around the red oval track, she felt lucky to be moving at all.

Nobody had made her do it. Terry, her coach, kept trying to send her to the showers to cool off, but Melissa couldn't stop. She wanted to run. Had to run. It was the only way she could get away from the painful memory of last night's dinner.

Melissa still felt her face flush with embarrassment every time she remembered how dowdy her parents had looked, and, how, between the two of them, they'd barely said a dozen words. But maybe that was for the best. At least, her father's drinking problem wasn't public knowledge. Or was it?

Even though Scott had prevented a crisis by whisking away the champagne bottle—and for that, Melissa was very grateful—the rest of the evening had been painful and uncomfortable. The McDormands had turned down Sue's invitation to go out drinking, and Sue had looked relieved rather than disappointed.

After the cake, Melissa, Brooks, and their parents had taken a short walking tour of the campus, where no one said a word until they reached the parking lot. Then it seemed as if the Baldwins couldn't get into their car fast enough, and Melissa's parents made a run for the bus stop.

Lovely as Brooks's parents were, they couldn't have missed what was so painfully obvious. Melissa's family was beneath them. They'd probably spent the whole ride home wondering how they could talk Brooks out of marrying into such a family of losers.

Melissa fell farther behind as she came around the curve into the back stretch. Even with all her potential, she'd probably end up the way the rest of her family had—in last place. But she had to fight it as long as she could. Summoning her last bit of strength, Melissa forced her exhausted legs to pump harder, and she pulled ahead, back into the pack. Caitlin Bruneau, the leader, was just a few yards ahead now, within striking distance.

Melissa tried to find her kick, to pour on that last bit of speed the way she had so many times while Brooks stood on the sidelines, cheering her on. Brooks wasn't there now. In fact, Melissa had no idea where he was. They'd hardly said a word to each other last night, and she hadn't seen or spoken to him all day.

Of course, that was mostly her own fault. She'd been hiding out at the track just so she wouldn't have to see him. But she couldn't keep this up forever. Already, she was falling behind again as they reached the final curve, heading for the last straightaway. Melissa staggered, gasping across the finish line, tied for last place.

So what had she proven today? That she was good at hiding? She certainly hadn't set any middle distance records. All she'd really shown herself was what a coward she was. Brooks didn't deserve that. He deserved warmth and attention, not icy stares and embarrassed silences. What kind of a wife would she make if she kept that up? And how long would Brooks even want her to be his wife if she acted that way?

Still sucking in air, and pressing her hands against her aching lower back, Melissa finally headed for the locker rooms.

"McDormand!" Terry's voice called after her. "You have a visitor."

Melissa turned, surprised. Had Brooks come to watch practice after all? She searched the field, filled with sprinters, shot-putters, and pole vaulters, for the glint of gold on Brooks's blond curls. But all she saw was a heavyset woman in too-tight pants, marching straight toward her.

It took Melissa a second to recognize her own mother. What was she doing here? Melissa briefly considered making a last dash to the locker room, but her legs wouldn't carry her. Anyway, it was too late. Her mother had already caught her eye.

"Hi, Ma," Melissa said, feeling more guilt overwhelm her. Now that she was looking into her mother's tired face, she was reminded of how hard her mother had always worked to support the family. She was reminded of how proud her mother had always been of Melissa's accomplishments, even though Melissa rarely made any effort to include her in her life. Melissa's mother hadn't said a word yet, and already Melissa felt the tears welling in her eyes.

"You got a minute?" her mother asked.

"Sure, Ma," Melissa said, nodding toward the

empty bleachers. "You want to sit down?"

Mrs. McDormand nodded, and the two silently made their way past a group of girls stretching at the side of the track. When they'd sat down on the hard wooden bench of the first row, Melissa's mother surveyed the field. "This place is big," she said.

Melissa felt another stab of guilt. This was the first time her mother had even seen the track. Melissa had been at U. of S. almost a year, and she'd never invited her parents to watch her run a single race. Not that her father would have come, of course. He never left the house. Melissa had been totally shocked he'd managed to make it to the dinner last night. But her mother might have come, when she wasn't working.

"So why didn't you say something?" her mother asked, still looking out at the field.

"Say something about what?" Melissa could tell her mother was finally getting down to business, but Melissa didn't have the slightest idea what she was talking about.

Melissa's mother looked at her with weary eyes. "The champagne. Last night. I could see the look on your face. You were afraid of what would happen if that kid opened the bottle in front of your father."

"You're darn right I was scared," Melissa said. "Weren't you? You know how Dad acts once he gets going. He would have started insulting the

Baldwins, calling them rich capitalists or oppressors or whatever babble came off the top of his head. Then he'd probably have begged Brooks's father for a job or told Sue she has great legs."

"No," Mrs. McDormand said.

"No? No what?"

"No, I wasn't scared."

"Well, you should have been."

"How would you know how I should have been?" Melissa's mother demanded. "You don't have the slightest idea what's going on."

"I don't know what you're talking about," Melissa said, beginning to feel irritated. What was her mother yelling at her for? Melissa wasn't the one with the drinking problem.

"That's right, you don't," Mrs. McDormand snapped. "You were so busy last night being ashamed of us that you never bothered to figure out what was really going on. It wouldn't have mattered one bit whether or not the champagne had been poured. Your father's on the wagon."

Melissa felt a lurching sensation in her stomach. She couldn't have heard right. Her father hadn't gone a day without booze for as long as she'd been alive.

"I know it's hard to believe," her mother said, "but it's true. He hasn't touched a drop in over six months."

"Six months?" Melissa asked, feeling the bench beneath

her start to spin. "How come . . . how come . . ."

"How come we never told you? When would we have said something? All those times you called us at home to let us know how you're doing? Or maybe that time you came to visit with your girlfriends?"

Melissa clutched the bench beneath her and tried not to cry. Her mother was right. Melissa hadn't made any effort to get in touch with her parents. She was too busy pretending they didn't exist. "I'm sorry," she said in a whisper.

"I know," said Mrs. McDormand. "But sorry isn't enough. You can treat us this way. We'll always be your parents, no matter what happens. But husbands don't have to stick around."

"You mean Brooks," Melissa said, wondering how her mother knew there was a problem between Brooks and her.

"Of course I mean Brooks," Mrs. McDormand said. "It's no different with husbands than parents. Brooks seems like a solid, caring person. But if you want your marriage to have a chance, you'd better be more open with him than you are with us. Otherwise, you're in for serious trouble."

That afternoon, Liza trudged along the hard-packed earth of the bicycle path that ran around Mill

Pond. The renovated University Theater was just around the bend and hanging in the lobby was the list of names that would end two weeks of personal and professional torture. The cast list for *Macbeth* was up.

One of the drama majors in her dorm had come screaming down the hall to announce it, and half of Coleridge Hall had emptied out as people raced over to find out who'd get the honor of working with the great Lawrence Briscoe. Liza wasn't running, though. Why should she? She hadn't shown up for her callback or casting couch session or whatever it was going to be. There was no way Briscoe had cast her as Lady Macbeth.

On the other hand, maybe there was still a chance she'd get the part. No matter what Briscoe really wanted from the girls at U. of S., he couldn't cast a no-talent. He still had his reputation to consider. And what better way to get good notices than to cast the girl who was *born* to play Lady Macbeth? Liza was certain no other actress on campus could have given a reading half as good as her's. Could Briscoe really pass up this opportunity to say he was the one who'd discovered Liza Ruff?

Liza could see the theater. It was an old building made of gray stone, with wide marble steps. The steps led up to several pairs of arched oak doors, which had replaced the old battered ones.

It looked almost more like a place of worship than a theater, a place where soon audiences would come to worship *her*, to throw roses at her feet. Breaking into a run, Liza cut through the woods and took the stairs two at a time. What had she been so depressed for? This was going to be her lucky day.

When Liza blasted through the middle pair of doors, she saw right away where the list was because a huge crowd of people was huddled around it. As Liza approached, she waited for everyone to whisper and point to her jealously. But they all seemed too mesmerized by the piece of paper thumbtacked to the brand new bulletin board.

Pushing through the mass of bodies, Liza squinted to read the typewritten names.

"Lady Macbeth, Lady Macbeth," she murmured, scanning the list of dramatis personae. There it was! Right after "An Old Man." Lady Macbeth was going to be played by—

"Erin Grant?" Liza cried out disbelievingly. How could this be? Liza had seen Erin perform recently in a production of *Uncle Vanya,* and "wooden" would have been a generous way to describe her performance. Erin had been flat and one-dimensional, relying solely on her husky voice, as if sounding good could make up for a total lack of acting ability.

There had to be some mistake. Maybe it was a

typo. Liza's name had to be up there. Checking the list again, Liza smiled in relief. There it was. Liza Ruff. Right after the words "Third Witch." Faith's name was up there too, as the prop person.

Liza's body suddenly felt very heavy. She wanted to sink to the floor and just stay there in a heap. What a waste of her talent. All the third witch did was agree with the first two and say "Hail" a couple of times. Whoever said there were no small parts, only small actors had never read *Macbeth*.

"I can't believe it either," a girl near Liza was whispering to the guy next to her. "Did you see her in *Uncle Vanya*? She was absolutely dreadful!"

Liza perked up a little. At least she wasn't alone in her opinion.

"How could Briscoe have cast her as Lady Macbeth?" the guy asked. "Everyone in the drama department knows she's a stiff."

"I hear she was pretty loose the other night," the girl said meaningfully, wiggling her eyebrows. "I hear she and Briscoe had a private casting session, if you know what I mean."

The guy nodded. "I figured it had to be something like that."

Liza felt like a total idiot. How could she have been so naive? How could she have thought, even for a split second, that Briscoe would cast her without seeing her "passion for theater"? Faith had been absolutely right about him, after all.

Liza was starting to feel claustrophobic. Breaking out of the crowd, she left the lobby and sat down on the top step outside the front doors. The air was cooler than it had been in weeks, rustling the leaves in the small woods that surrounded the theater. In the distance, Liza could hear the sounds of splashing water and happy screams coming from nearby Mill Pond.

People were still streaming up the steps of the theater, their faces filled with hope and anxiety, but for Liza it was all over. Thanks to her high scruples, she was going to be totally insignificant up on stage, while undeserving Erin got all the attention. Liza was almost sure the situation would have been reversed if she'd kept her date with Briscoe. Had Liza been a fool for giving up such an important opportunity?

Or was she just a fool in general? Faith certainly seemed to think so. It didn't matter what Liza did anymore, Faith was determined to hate her. Liza didn't know how much longer she could live this way. The cold stares. The uncomfortable silences. The constant fights. Liza couldn't even go back to her room to hide from the cruelty in the world. There was no place and no one to comfort her in her disappointment.

Liza jumped as something cold and wet pushed against her hand. "Wha—?" Then she looked down and saw that Max, the dorm mutt, had climbed the stairs and was nuzzling her affectionately with his nose. He wore a red bandanna around his scruffy neck, and his brown eyes stared at her with love.

It was the look in his eyes that did it. No living creature had looked at her with so much affection since she'd arrived at U. of S. Liza threw her arms around the dog. "Oh, Max," she sobbed, as the tears sprang from her eyes. Her tears fell against the soft golden fur of Max's shoulder, but the dog didn't seem to mind. He just sat there patiently and licked Liza's tearstained face.

KC could still see those glossy travel brochures, fluttering in Winnie's outstretched hand. She'd been seeing those brochures in her mind's eye for the past twenty-four hours. KC had always thought Winnie's ideas were off the wall, but not anymore. Now KC was convinced that Winnie was a genius.

"This place is so beautiful," Peter said as he and KC walked hand in hand through the woods surrounding Mill Pond. "I don't know how I'm ever going to be able to leave. Or maybe it just seems beautiful because you're with me."

KC, stepping through the mulch of wet leaves, twigs, and damp earth, tried to bring her mind back to the woods. She breathed in the fresh smell of the rustling green canopy overhead. It was so peaceful here, so dark and quiet. If she closed her eyes and screened out the splashing sounds of a water fight on Mill Pond, she could almost pretend that she and Peter were the only two people in the world, and that the world extended only to the edge of the woods. Then it wouldn't matter if Peter traveled to the other end of the world. He'd always be nearby.

But that wasn't the only way she and Peter could stay close. Those brochures of Winnie's had started an idea brewing in her mind. It was an idea that would turn KC's whole life upside down and take Peter completely by surprise, but KC couldn't let go of it.

"You're so quiet," Peter observed, pulling KC close and stroking her dark curls.

KC gazed steadily into Peter's hazel eyes. In the shadows of the woods, they appeared much darker, almost forest green. His face looked as calm as she felt inside. They'd moved beyond the intensity of the past few weeks to a higher state of being. It was almost as if their souls had joined and words were no longer necessary.

Almost. There was no way Peter could know about her crazy idea.

"Tell me," Peter said, guessing everything but the thought itself. "You won't stop thinking about it until you do."

"You're right," KC said, dropping her eyes. "I'm just not sure how you'll take it."

"Try me," Peter said, gently stroking her face with the back of his hand.

KC took another breath of the fresh air and tried to draw strength from it. "I was thinking," she said, forcing her eyes to find his again, "what if I went to Europe to study, too? I could talk to my Grandma Rose and see if she'd be willing to pay for my expenses. She always told me she wanted to go to Europe when she was my age, but her family didn't have the money to send her. And I could find a part-time job. But maybe it's a really bad idea. You probably think I'm just tagging along or trying to steal your thunder."

Peter silenced her by laying his fingertip against her lips.

"I'm sorry," KC said. "I guess I should just let you go gracefully, huh?"

Peter suddenly grabbed KC with a force that would have knocked her off her feet if he weren't holding on to her so tightly. Then he pressed his mouth against hers and kissed her long and hard. "There's my answer," he said, finally drawing back.

KC stared at him, feeling a little giddy. "Does that mean you like the idea?" she asked.

"Like it?" Peter shouted so loud that unseen birds began to twitter in response. "I love it! Just the way I love you!"

Sixteen

Tick! Tick! Tick!

The clock on the cinder block wall of the student union waiting room kept quartz time, jerking forward second by second instead of flowing smoothly. Each tick sounded like a drop of water hitting Faith on the head, pushing her closer to the moment when she'd have to face the peer review board.

Tick! Tick! Tick!

Faith stared at the stark white walls, bare of any pictures or decoration, in keeping with school regulations. There were two gray metal doors, one leading into the tribunal hall, and one leading out to the main corridor. The only furnishings were the wooden bench she sat on and one just like it on the other side of the room. It looked as if she was already in prison. Was this just a hint of what was to come?

Tick! Tick! Tick!

Faith could picture the dimly lit room on the other side of the interior door. The long table. Three grim faces peering at her, probing her, beating her down with questions until she begged for mercy. *Yes!* she'd scream. *I'm guilty! I don't deserve to live.*

Or at least not live on campus as a regular student. She'd given up that right when Erin had written the citation for Liza's burning candles. This minor infraction on top of her probation meant her parents would have to come in, not to mention half a dozen other penalties the board could slap her with. Total suspension from all extracurricular activities. Community service cleaning up garbage dumped illegally in vacant lots. Perpetual kitchen duty in the dining commons.

Faith knew she should be happy that at least she hadn't been cited for the champagne. Punishment for that would have been total expulsion. But she was still really scared. What if they told her she couldn't work on any more plays? She'd have to give up being a drama major. If that happened, she might as well be expelled.

Tick! Tick! Tick!

Maybe that would make life easier anyway, now that she owed Briscoe a debt. His insinuations still made her shiver. Exactly how was he planning to collect—with a pound of flesh? It sure looked that way after she'd seen the cast list. Briscoe was only interested in one thing, and Erin must have given it to him.

Tick! Tick! Tick!

What it all boiled down to, once again, was the fact that there were so many Mr. Wrongs in her life. Even with her checklist, they kept finding ways to sneak up on her.

"Am I late?" A cheerful voice broke through the oppressive atmosphere, and the door opened.

"Scott!" Faith cried, smiling despite everything.

Scott was a splash of color against the bare white wall. He wore fluorescent yellow-and-orange baggy shorts that came down to his knees and a bright red football jersey that had been cut off to reveal several inches of his well-defined abdominal muscles. His shaggy hair framed his tan, smiling face.

"What are you late for?" Faith asked. "Do you have to go in front of the board, too?"

"Of course not," Scott said, plopping down on the bench next to Faith. "I'm here to give moral support."

"To me?"

"Of course to you!" He put his arm around her shoulder and pulled her close.

Mr. Wrong or no, Faith couldn't deny that she was happy to see him. She felt less scared, less alone, sheltered here in the crook of his arm. But she couldn't understand what he was doing here. They were just two people who saw each other occasionally, without any commitment.

"I'll be waiting right here when you come out," Scott said. "You can cry on my shoulder, tell me what jerks they are, you can even tell me *I'm* a jerk if it will make you feel better."

"You're not a jerk." The words were out of Faith's mouth before she realized she'd said them. But she didn't want to take them back. Despite what had happened with Briscoe and the champagne, Scott had really come through for her at the party.

Maybe there was something to be said for being spontaneous after all. Last night had made it clear that you couldn't plan for every situation. Sometimes things happened that you couldn't predict. And when they did, you had to be flexible. The way Scott was.

"You know, I never got to thank you for what you did last night," Faith said. "I still don't understand why you went out of your way to help me. You're so confusing, sometimes."

"What do you mean?" Scott asked.

"Well, sometimes you're there for me, like yesterday and right now, and sometimes you just vanish into thin air. I never know what to expect from you."

Scott shrugged. "That's not confusing. That's just the way I am."

"Faith Crowley," a young woman called, opening the door to the tribunal hall. She wore a black blazer over a gray dress, and her face was pale and grim. Faith recognized her as one of the judges from her last peer review.

Faith swallowed painfully. For just a moment, Scott had almost made her forget where she was. But it was time to face the board. Faith stood up and tucked her blouse into her denim skirt.

"Good luck," Scott said, reaching out to squeeze her hand. He was smiling, but Faith could read the concern in his eyes. "Scream if you need help."

"Thanks," Faith said, taking in a shaky breath.

"Follow me, please," the young woman said, leading Faith into the same large, dimly lit room she'd been in so recently.

There were another young woman and a young man sitting at the far end of the room behind a long Formica table, each equipped with a notepad and a dog-eared copy of the U. of S. handbook. Faith recognized them, too, from her last review. They'd been so stern with her, so absolutely unforgiving, that she could only expect similar harsh treatment.

A plain wooden chair was set up in the empty space in front of the table. The rest of the room was absolutely bare.

"Please sit down," said the woman in the black blazer.

Faith sat down on the hard wooden chair.

"You're Faith Crowley," said the young man. "I remember you."

Faith held on to the sides of the chair to keep from trembling. This wasn't going to be a trial. They were going to skip straight to the conviction. They already knew she was Faith Crowley, Repeat Offender. They'd probably figured out her punishment before she stepped in the door. The only question now was—would she have any reason for living once they were through with her?

"So what's the charge?" the young man said, checking a typewritten list in front of him.

"Minor infraction," said the woman who'd ushered her in. "Candles burning in the room."

The man sighed. "Another one? Let me guess. Coleridge Hall?"

"You got it," the other woman, a blond, said. "Erin's up to her old tricks."

The man scowled. "What's the matter with her?

Does she think we have nothing better to do than sit around all day punishing people for making popcorn in their rooms?"

Faith wasn't sure she was hearing right. This guy seemed more angry with Erin than he was with her. Was this a good sign?

"We've got twenty more minors today alone," said the blond, "and they're *all* from Coleridge. Heating coils, posters tacked to the walls, and— get this—disrespect. Someone talked back to Erin, so she slapped them with a citation. I can't even find that one in the rule book."

"She must have made it up," said the man. "I think it's time we had a little talk with her."

"Ahem . . ." The woman with the black blazer cleared her throat and nodded toward Faith.

"Oh, right," said the young man, checking his list. "What was this, again? Candles?"

"Three burning candles in the room," read the blond from a copy of the citation. "Wax dripping onto school property. I guess that means the desk."

"Let me see that," said the man, taking the citation. He read it and looked up. "Faith Crowley," he said in an official-sounding voice.

"Yes?" Faith said, hoping her voice wasn't trembling too much.

"Here is the decision of the board."

Faith gulped. She'd been foolish to think their anger at Erin would somehow save her. If anything, the fact that they were upset would only make it that much worse for her. Judges were human beings, and angry human beings gave harsher punishments.

"The decision of the board is that you are free to go," said the man as he ripped the citation into tiny pieces and dropped them in the wastebasket behind him.

Faith just stared, dumbstruck. "Does this mean. . ."

The young man smiled. "It means the citation never happened. Have a nice day."

Nice day? This had to be the nicest day of her life. Faith practically leaped out of her seat. She felt like screaming at the top of her lungs, only that probably wouldn't look too good in front of the board. She'd have to wait until she got outside and told Scott the good news. Suddenly, she found that she couldn't wait to see him. Of all the people she knew, he was the one she most wanted to share this with.

"Thank you very much," Faith said, with a little bow. "I really appreciate this." Then she turned and ran.

"Well?" Scott asked. He'd been standing just a few inches from the door, so she nearly bumped into him.

Faith threw her arms around him and buried her

face in his strong chest. Then she grabbed his hand and led him out into the hallway.

"Where are we going?" Scott asked.

"Outside," Faith said as they pushed through the front doors. "I need some fresh air."

The air did smell incredibly fresh as they headed across the green. The heat wave had finally broken, and there was a brisk breeze blowing down from the distant mountains. The sun shone, but without the intensity of the past few weeks, and the green was filled with people playing Frisbee and touch football.

"Isn't it a beautiful day?" Faith asked, swinging Scott's hand like a little girl.

"You tell me," Scott said, pulling on her hand to make her stop walking. "How nice a day is it?"

"The best," Faith said, grabbing Scott's other hand as she faced him. "They ripped up my citation. It's not going to go on my record. I'm a free woman."

Scott's face lit up. "All right!" He grabbed Faith around the waist and swung her around and around until they both collapsed dizzily onto the grass. Then they both lay down and Faith rested her head against Scott's shoulder.

It felt so good to be with him. Not because she was madly in love or wanted to spend her life with him, but because he made her feel good *right now*. And that was all she needed, for the moment.

She'd tried to plan her life, to account for every possibility, but she was beginning to learn that life didn't always work out the way you thought it would. And relationships didn't always work that way either. How could you know, at eighteen, whether someone was right for you in the long run? Maybe Melissa and Brooks thought they did, but Faith had no idea what would happen to her next week, let alone ten years down the line.

So who cared whether Scott was Mr. Right or not? Maybe there was no such thing as a Mr. Right, just a person you wanted to be with at a particular time. And Scott was right for right now. They didn't have to have a heavy commitment. They could improvise. Sometimes they could be romantic. Other times they could just be friends. She would go with the flow.

Faith propped herself up on one elbow and planted a big wet kiss on Scott's mouth.

Scott's eyes sparkled. "What was that for?"

Faith shrugged. "I don't know. I just felt like doing it."

Scott laughed and pulled Faith down on top of him. "Sounds like a good reason."

Faith laughed, too, and tickled Scott's bare stomach with her fingertips. She wasn't going to worry about anything but right now. The future would take care of itself.

Here's a sneak preview of
Freshman Heartbreak, *the fifteenth*
book in the dramatic story of
FRESHMAN DORM.

I t's midnight," Winnie heard Melissa say.
"What are you planning to do?"

"What everyone does at this witchly
hour," Winnie said as she walked out of their
dorm room. "Jog."

She hurried down the stairs of Forest Hall and
out into the pitch black night. The air was a little
chilly so Winnie pumped her legs briskly and
headed toward the trees on the opposite side of
the quad. There wasn't a soul around.

Nothing like a little terror to get the adrenaline
going, Winnie assured herself. *I could start a new*
program for the athletic department: Fitness

Through Fear. It might catch on.

She ran down a hill and jumped over a low hedge that separated the quad from the athletic fields. Running along the back of the gym, and around the football stadium, she started on the footpath alongside the tennis courts. The nets gently flapped in the light wind and Winnie inhaled deeply. It was exciting being out here all by herself, moving through space like she owned it. There was something about running—not just the high she always got—but the complete freedom. When her body and brain were in perfect rhythm, she felt as if she could do no wrong.

Then she heard it. Her own footfalls sounded absolutely regular, but another set of feet had a different tempo. Someone was running behind her. *Phap, phap, breathe. Phap, phap, breathe.* Each slap on the ground came right after hers.

Despite what she'd told Melissa, it wasn't common to run into other joggers at this time of night. A sudden panic shot through her entire body.

God, Winnie, get out of here, she told herself. *This is the 90's for heaven's sake. Night joggers are prime targets.*

She ran faster, hoping to blot out the sound of the other runner, but when her speed picked up, so did his. It had to be a him. The footfalls were too heavy for another woman.

Without wanting to, Winnie turned briefly, hoping that the sounds weren't real. Maybe they were just paranoid hallucinations. But as soon as she looked back, Winnie spotted a tall man. It was too dark to see features, but she could tell from his shape that he was strong and well-built.

She bit her lip and said a small prayer, then really put on the speed.

"Hey, wait up!"

Oh, Mom, Winnie thought silently. *I'm sorry I had that big fight with you when I was thirteen. I mean, you were acting like such a single mother and such a shrink. I had to rebel. And I never did get my nose pierced anyhow, so what was it all about?* Then she thought about Josh. Would he miss her? Probably not. Lately he didn't seem to know she was alive.

"Come on, slow down. Give me a break."

It was impossible. He was right on her heels. Winnie gave another quick glance over her shoulder, and saw that the runner was wearing a U of S track suit, the same kind Melissa wore. Did that mean he belonged on campus? The thought made her feel only slightly better.

Then he was by her side, matching his rhythm to hers. "You really like sprinting, don't you?" he asked.

For a second, Winnie looked straight ahead, wondering if she could just keep him talking until they got to Greek Row. That would allow her to go and pound on the door of the Tri Beta sorority and scream bloody murder until someone woke up. Without breaking pace, she glanced sideways at him. He was grinning.

"I know you from somewhere," he said. "Do *I* look familiar?" His voice was mellow, hardly affected by the hard running, but Winnie could detect a hint of an accent she couldn't place.

"I don't know you," Winnie said. "Could you leave me alone, please?"

"Wait a second, I'll figure it out."

"Figure what out?" Winnie gasped as she tripped over a crack in the pavement.

"I have total recall. It's not Western Civ, is it?"

Winnie ran faster.

"And it's not that big poli sci course. Sure, I can pin you exactly." He reached over and grabbed her wrist. She wheeled around and jerked to a halt beside him just as they made it off-campus, onto the Springfield street that led into town. Standing next to him, she suddenly felt very small and terribly weak. There wasn't a car or person in sight. Her knees began to buckle.